Peal
C

P9-CFL-022

Ella
Mental

And the Good Sense Guide

YP PAPER DECKERS
Deckers, Amber.
Ella mental : and the good
sense guide / Amber Deckers.

MAR 2 1 '06

DISCARD

DISCARD

Ella Mental

Mental

And the Good Sense Guide

Amber Deckers

Peabody Public Library
Columbia City, IN

Simon Pulse
New York   London   Toronto   Sydney

If you purchased this book without a cover, you should be aware that this book is stolen property. It was reported as "unsold and destroyed" to the publisher, and neither the author nor the publisher has received any payment for this "stripped book."

This book is a work of fiction. Any references to historical events, real people, or real locales are used fictitiously. Other names, characters, places, and incidents are the product of the author's imagination, and any resemblance to actual events or locales or persons, living or dead, is entirely coincidental.

SIMON PULSE
An imprint of Simon & Schuster Children's Publishing Division
1230 Avenue of the Americas, New York, NY 10020

Copyright © 2005 by Amber Deckers
Originally published in Great Britain in 2005 by Orchard Books
Published by arrangement with Orchard Books
All rights reserved, including the right of reproduction in whole or in part in any form.

SIMON PULSE and colophon are registered trademarks of Simon & Schuster, Inc.

The text of this book was set in Goudy.

Manufactured in the United States of America
First Simon Pulse edition April 2006
10 9 8 7 6 5 4 3

Library of Congress Control Number 2005931306
ISBN-13: 978-1-4169-1322-1
ISBN-10: 1-4169-1322-X

For Craig— my love and my light

Chapter 1
Hatching Plans

At this very moment Toby is lying belly-down on the floor, staring intently at his English workbook and doing strange jerky things with his legs as if he's being mysteriously electrocuted. I'm spread out on the couch, alternately staring at Toby and my English workbook. So far I've written the words "Human Relationships" at the top of the lined sheet of paper, but nothing else. A 500-word essay on human relationships: That's this week's homework, set by our English teacher Miss O'Connor. We've been studying poets like William Blake and Robert Burns and learning how "their personal relationships form the basis for their writing," and now we're supposed to do the same—write about how our loved ones influence our lives. I usually quite like this sort of thing. Most girls do, I reckon—we're far more in touch with our inner feelings than boys, although today even I'm struggling. It all seems very intense for a Thursday afternoon.

Peabody Public Library
Columbia City, IN

Toby really isn't into anything academic and hates books and reading. People say I'm the brainy one, but that's only because I'm a closet book-worm and secretly enjoy schoolwork and learning, although I have enough sense not to advertise this geeky fact and always make a point of looking bored in class. Toby's really quite bright too, but he simply can't sit still for very long and would rather be out on a field chasing a ball. He almost failed last term, so it's up to me to make sure that he passes the looming exams. We've set a studying schedule, which Toby agreed to at first but now growls about constantly. I would just die if he failed and stayed behind a year!

Toby is my soul mate and truly one of a kind. He's down-to-earth and honest and genuinely doesn't give a rat's shalala what other people think about him. Some people like to pretend that they don't care but spend hours agonizing over who is saying what about them, but Toby really does not care. He's super cool. Add this to the fact that he's tall, well-built and a top-notch footy player and it's easy to understand why he's one of the most popular blokes at Dunton Secondary, which is where we go to school. As we're best mates, I wish this meant that I'm also really popular, but unfortunately I think I'm tolerated rather than appreciated. And I'm tolerated because it's like an unspoken rule with Toby. If you want to be mates with him you have to be mates with me too. Bless the saints and their robes for Toby.

"Hey, a deal's a deal!" I whinge, desperately wishing he would take this homework assignment seriously. Toby scrunches up his face and gives me a look which says "haggard old witch" and is obviously meant to offend me but misses its target entirely (although if he asks me where I've parked my broom once more I'm definitely throwing something sharp at him). "I hope the wind changes and you stay like that forever," I sigh, trying to sound uninterested.

Toby's legs are now jerking in time with the drumming sound he's making with his pen on his open book, which is making it difficult to concentrate. My sanity fractures. "TOBY!" I finally snap. "You are driving me bleedin' barmy! We said we would study until four—do you want to be a dummy for the rest of your life?" I wouldn't normally call Toby a dummy, but desperate times call for desperate measures.

"So you reckon that writing soppy essays for

Miss O'Connor is going to make me smart, huh?" he asks, puffing at the curtain of blond fringe that's fallen across his bright blue eyes.

Mmm . . . he has a point, I think to myself (but would never let on). Toby continues eyeballing me and begins blowing glistening spitbubbles at the same time. Yuk! He's thoroughly enjoying my baffled silence.

"Well, put it this way Toby," I finally respond, "you have to write soppy essays to write your term exam. And if you don't write the term exam . . . you fail! Get it? Got it? Good! Now nobody said it had to be award-winning stuff, just write whatever comes into your pip so that we can get out of here."

To drive my point home I quickly start scribbling whatever words come into my own head. I don't glance up until I've finally filled an entire page, and when I do I'm glad to see that Toby is busily writing too. His tongue is rolled out halfway across his cheek, which is a sure sign that he's concentrating.

Toby and I have been best friends for as long as we've been walking upright, but we're also two of a group of really good mates. We're not like a gang or a crew with a street name or anything daft

4

like that; we're just a bunch of kids who enjoy hanging out together. We were all friends at primary school and now that we're insignificant froth on the pond that is Dunton Secondary, it just seems natural that we should stick together. This afternoon we're meeting up at the park near the cinema complex. Everyone calls it the cinema complex but Dunton, which is where we live, is rather a small town and the cinema complex really only consists of a fake-French-style bakery, a moldy laundrette, a small bank, a second-hand bookshop called Bookends, and a fifty-seater cinema that's always showing last month's movie. Nothing very complex about that, but then who am I to break with tradition?

"Right, we're off!" Toby suddenly barks, tossing his pen into the air and leaping towards the coat rack in one unbroken movement.

It's wintertime so we need jackets, although it's not the cold I mind as much as the permanent ceiling of heavy grey cloud that hangs overhead and the darkness that comes calling far too early. I love summertime, when it's always light and there's enough time for everything—and you don't have to defrost your toes with the hairdryer.

Toby is already halfway out the door and

performing clever maneuvres with his football, so I make a grab for my coat and head out after him.

"What time do you have to be back?" he asks.

"Back where?" I mumble absently, still struggling into my jacket.

"To Mars, space girl!" he scoffs. "Back home, where else?"

"Oh, you mean hell? Normal time, I guess," I sigh despondently.

Toby shakes his head. "Your parental units soooo need to chill out."

"Thanks for the reminder," I brood.

Toby flicks the ball my way, but as usual I miss and have to run to catch it. I have the ball skills of a deboned chicken, but I don't mind looking stupid in front of Toby and attempt to dribble the ball slowly along the pavement.

"Keep your eye on the ball!" Toby shouts.

"Keep your eye on my butt!" I yell in return, pretending to be annoyed and quickly pelting the ball his way. Of course it veers in the complete opposite direction and Toby has to sprint to catch it before it disappears down the embankment. He thinks this is very funny, so I point my tongue at him and we walk in silence to the park.

Our silences are never strained, which I think

is a sign of a good friendship. Sometimes I have a million things to say, other times I simply like to watch the world go by. Gran says that God gave us two ears but only one mouth, which I think translates to mean that we should listen more than we talk—but then this is coming from a woman who uses purple hair rinse and is convinced that Elvis has been reincarnated as Pogo, her wire-haired Jack Russell. He can, after all, howl the chorus to "Are You Lonesome Tonight" without missing a beat. There's no arguing with this sort of bent logic.

In winter when the trees are stripped bare of their leaves you can see right across the valley to the outskirts of London, and the view is spectacular. Toby can't wait to get lost in the big city, but I love living in a small town. Even if you don't know what you're doing somebody else always does, and I find that strangely comforting.

A dark shape moves up ahead. "Tom!" I holler through cupped hands, recognizing our friend. The figure spins in fright, raising his fists defensively and frowning. He's usually really chilled and I can't imagine what's lit his fuse, but the instant he recognizes us, he smiles. Toby expertly lobs the ball towards our gangly friend, who just as skilfully heads it and catches it.

"Hey, Tom-Tom," I sing. When Tom was younger he had a slight stutter, and from this stutter came the nickname Tom-Tom. But only his good friends call him this and it's meant as an affectionate pet name, never as a taunt.

"We give you a bit of a scare, tough guy?" Toby asks, giving him a hearty wallop on the back.

"You never know who's lurking around the corner!" Tom-Tom grins, but his lips are taut with a peculiar uneasiness I don't remember seeing before.

Tom and Toby start fooling around with the football and leave me standing in the road like Norma No-Mates, but luckily we're almost at the park where Frannie is sitting with Alf and Pearl. I jog over and collapse on the grass just as Alf jumps to his feet and dashes over to where the other two boys are behaving like toddlers with the ball.

"Was it something I said?" I slot myself in closer between Fran and Pearl.

"Hiya, sweetie!" Frannie smiles. "Must we keep reminding you that when there's a football involved you, along with the rest of the population, are invisible. You're dinosaur dust!" she jokes, rolling her eyes dramatically. "I wish I were a bloke. A patch of green grass and a bit of leather pumped full of air and they're happy."

"Yeah, but how interesting can that be?" exclaims Pearl. "It's much more fun being a girl: Not only do you get to gossip about everybody and grow breasticles, but you can use blemish stick to cover your zits without people thinking you're a sorry sister."

The word breasticles really is mine, I think to myself. I was—after all—the one who heard it first, but like salt Pearl adds it to everything. She is the raunchy one I suppose and I don't have copyright on it, so there you go.

"But enough about those blokes," Pearl continues, "get this: Michael is sort of having a party tomorrow night!" Squeal. Pause. "We are all going, aren't we?"

"What does 'sort of having a party' mean?" I ask skeptically. Michael is Pearl's new boyfriend and we all think he's a spanner, but we don't want to hurt her feelings and so keep our opinions far from her ears. Not that she'd listen to a word we said anyway.

"Well, he's not like having a party with loads of people, but his folks are visiting his sister in Cambridge so we're invited to go and hang out at his place," explains Pearl, her eyes shimmering with excitement.

This is a flop-proof recipe for disaster, my inner voice pipes up. Pearl is the eldest of four kids and lives with her mum, sister, two brothers, and grandmother in a council house. She's always complaining how she hates her life and lives for the day when she can escape Dunton forever. I think if Pearl got more attention at home she'd be happier, because she really is a good person. She just needs to be noticed and cuddled and loved more than most. Her problem is that she looks for love in all the wrong places, and generally in the clutches of the wrong sort of bloke. Pearl is a year older than me and I know that she's not a virgin any more; it's obvious by the type of blokes she goes with. They're usually a few years older and always seem to like her more when the lights are off. But Pearl doesn't seem to mind. Just as long as she's somebody's girlfriend.

"Don't you mean that you're invited?" I ask, not believing for one millisecond that Michael would want us there.

Pearl shrugs. "I've already told Michael that if he wants me in his life he'll have to accept that I have other friends too," she says. "So of course you're invited. It'll be such fun, you'll see!"

Frannie bounces her shoulders and I sit there

limply. "Um, you know what my folks are like," I say. They don't know exactly what my folks are like, but they have a general idea.

"You can tell them you're staying at my house," Frannie says half-heartedly, not ready to commit to the party but not wanting to leave me swinging either. I'm not allowed to sleep over at Toby's any more; mum says it has everything to do with our being teenagers. After Toby, Frannie is definitely my next best friend. She's utterly together with everything and has it all: brains, looks, cool parents, clear skin. If she wasn't my friend I think I'd definitely hate her.

"What do the guys think?" I ask Pearl.

"Tom-Tom says 'whatever,' which is his answer to everything, Alf is keen, and I haven't spoken to Toby yet," she answers.

As if on cue, the three lads come hurtling along and crumple down on the grass between us—red in the face and shiny from their game. Pearl immediately launches into another bubbly description of Michael's so-called party, all the while gazing up at Toby like a puppy begging for a biscuit.

"Sure, why not," Toby casually replies once her jaws have come to a standstill.

"You want to go?" I choke with disbelief.

"Yeah, all right then," he confirms.

Toby dislikes Michael just as much as I do and I suspect that he's saying this just to keep Pearl's smile in place. None of us trust the crazy, mean glint in Michael's eye—it's like he's not scared of anything and daring anybody to put it to the test. Alf sometimes gets a similar glint in his eye, but without the meanness. He seems to recognize that there is an invisible line between right and wrong and even when he's teetering on the very edge of it, he knows where to stop. He's over-excitable, is our Alfie—not nasty. But there's no telling what Michael is capable of; with him there just is no line.

We hang out together for a while and as usual I'm the first to leave, but not by choice. "I've got to leg it home," I say. Luckily I don't live far.

"Yeah right, see you tomorrow," says Toby.

"Cheerio," adds Frannie.

"Oh, Tobes," I say, remembering my homework, "don't forget my English workbook. I left it at your house and I'm mincemeat if I don't hand it in tomorrow!" Toby nods vaguely and I can see that he's not really listening. "And I might be late in the morning," I add, "I've got to get my eyes gouged out first."

Toby nods again. "Cool, no prob, Ellie."

He hasn't heard a word I've said and I give him a playful slap on the head. "I'll text you a reminder in the morning, mullet!" I chirp.

Toby is the only person who calls me Ellie and the fact that he cares enough about me to change my name so slightly makes me toasty. So I share the name with big, fat elephants the world over, but I've managed to overlook this narky little fact. My birth certificate states that my full name is Ella (no-middle-name) Watson, and I was born fourteen years and eight months ago. So Ella isn't short for anything. It's just Ella. Simple. When mum found out she was pregnant she decided to call her baby Anna, after my grandmother. But when she found out she was carrying twins she had to come up with another name, and quickly. She couldn't have one twin with a name and leave the other anonymous. That would be unfair—even to a fetus. So she named me after Ella Fitzgerald, her favorite singer of all time. But I don't look a thing like Ella Fitzgerald; she's black and I'm very white, so white in fact that in winter I'm more like a mottled shade of blue, which isn't very attractive. I'm always really envious of Tom-Tom's complexion in that respect - whatever the weather, his skin's always a warm brown. My hair is a light brown color and matches my eyes, which may sound like a nice combination—but unfortunately I just look like I've been put through a rinse cycle once too often. "Dull and drab": It's not a look that's made any *CosmoGIRL!* headlines lately.

Thursday afternoon means Dad is playing darts at the pub, which thankfully gives me a chance to ask Mum if I can sleep over at Frannie's tomorrow night. My parental units are equally strict, but my chances of getting the nod are far better if I catch one of them alone. Mum is in the kitchen feeding our dog, Trixie, which—in my opinion—is a really idiotic name, even for an odd-looking dog like this one. But Anna thought it was "cute" and so we're stuck with it. Most of the time I just call her "Dog" (Trixie—not my sister), but that's more to annoy Anna than anything else. Annoying Anna is one of my preferred pastimes. It's just as well we don't share any classes or a crowd at school, because that would make it a full-time job. Not that Anna actually has a crowd; her and her best mate Marcia just sort of flit about and get on with their own thing. They're public-school wannabees with state-school pockets, but still they think that they're one step up from the rest of us.

"Would it be all right if I stayed over at Frannie's tomorrow night?" I ask Mum nice-as-pie, giving Dog a scratch behind the ears.

"And hello to you too, Ella," mutters Mum with her brow all tied up in a scowl. I wonder if all mothers are as irritating as this one.

"Oh, hi Mum," I add cheerfully. "So, can I?"

Mum does like Frannie's folks, which improves my chances considerably. Of course I know that theoretically I'm lying by omission, but it's much better than lying outright. After all, I really will be putting my head on a pillow, closing my eyes and going to sleep in Frannie's house. I'm just failing to mention what's happening before the sleeping part. If I categorically stated that I wasn't doing anything else except sleeping at Frannie's, now *that* would be lying. Anyway, it's not my fault my parents don't trust me. It's not like I've given them any real reason not to.

"Yes, fine," she mutters eventually. Mum's head is in another time zone.

Suddenly the door springs open and ricochets off the wall. "Hello girls!" Dad croons. He seems to be in a good mood at least. He pitches his keys at the kitchen table and moves over to Mum, clutching her waist with his hairy fingers.

"Hello darling," Mum grins and sticks a kiss on his stubbly cheek. "I'm so glad you're home. Are you hungry?"

I am completely incapable of stomaching their lovey-dovey scenes before dinner and quietly slip upstairs to the sanctuary of my bedroom before he has a chance to reply.

Chapter 2
With a Rebel Yell

We hand in our English homework on "Human Relationships" and Toby appears relieved that for once he doesn't have to conjure up some stringy excuse for not having done his. He must be almost out of excuses by now, I should imagine. The rest of the day is uneventful and dawdles by, and as I sit staring at the ticking classroom clock, waiting for the final bell to sound, I contemplate the brain-freeze-boring life I lead. Mum says that these are the best years of my life. Thank goodness I don't believe much of what she says. We've been passing notes finalizing our plans for the evening. Pearl is racing home to begin primping, which should take up most of the afternoon, and the boys are off for a game of footy, which leaves Fran and me.

When do you want to fetch some clothes? she scrawls on a torn shred of paper.

Straight after school? I write below this and pass it back to her. That's the end of the notes so I guess she's happy with this arrangement.

We reach my house before three so Mum is still at work. She's an administrator at a nearby textile factory, although I don't really know exactly what an administrator does. Opening the front door I can hear schmaltzy music wafting down from upstairs, which can only mean that Anna is home. That, or Dog has become a secret boyband fan.

"I'm hungry," I notify Frannie. I'm always hungry and think there may be something physically wrong with me. Like maybe the bottom of my stomach is missing. Mum says I should practice a little of what she calls "self-control," but I've got to find it before I can practice it. I think my self-control went missing along with the bottom of my stomach.

"How does cheese and jam sound?" I ask, placing the doorstop-sliced Hovis on the kitchen counter and deciding to listen to the growl of my belly instead of the nagging voice (could that be my self-control?) in my head. Frannie nods, gulping down a glass of water. She's really good like that—always eating fresh fruit and drinking at least eight glasses of water a day. She says it's excellent for flushing out toxins, but all it does is leave me with clenched butt cheeks, nervously searching for the nearest loo.

Anna explodes into the kitchen, waving a razor in front of her like a sword. She likes a dramatic entrance, does our hoity-toity Anna. And she's even worse when I have a mate around. I think she thinks they're impressed by her. As if!

"Have you been using my razor again, Ella?" she yells accusingly.

"Who me?" I simper, putting on my innocent face.

"Yes YOU!" she roars louder. "I told you not to use my razor to shave your flaming legs, didn't I!"

"What makes you think I have used your razor?" I ask reasonably.

"These . . . ," she splutters, "are not mine!" One of her carefully manicured fingernails is pointing to a sprinkling of short hairs scattered on the shiny razor blade.

"And I suppose that you don't shave? Or maybe you just let your hair grow like a yeti!" I taunt her. Neither of us is allowed to shave, but of course we both do.

"This is my brand new razor, so it's obviously your gross-out hair, Ella!" she replies, but I refuse to dignify her insult with a response and continue silently spreading margarine on the Hovis slices. "Argh! It's pointless trying to talk to you. Loser!"

Anna finally shrieks and stomps from the kitchen like she's in training for the military.

"You're very vocal for someone who is not-even-allowed-to-shave-her-legs!" I screech after her.

"You're not allowed to shave your legs?" Frannie asks, staring holes in the Cheddar she's slicing.

"Not until we're sixteen," I grunt dismissively, feeling a bit bad that I've upset Anna but annoyed that she had to make a scene about a stupid razor. A girl's got to do what a girl's got to do, doesn't she?

Luckily for Anna we're not identical twins, although people say that if you stare hard through squinted eyes you can tell that we've shared a womb. If you stare hard through squinted eyes you'll see just about whatever you want to see, I reckon. My sister definitely has the looks in the family. She's got Dad's creamy skin and hair that's at least two shades lighter than mine, which makes her almost blonde—and blonde equals babe to most of the gormless geeks at Dunton Secondary. I think Mother Nature is having a bit of a laugh at my expense, to be honest. The whole purpose of being a twin is that you've got someone just like you. You look alike, you act alike; it's the pair of you pitted against the rest of the wicked world come sleet or sunshine! But our Anna toffs about like she's a supermodel, flicking her golden locks this way and that and walking with a swing that would be better off on a golf course. And worse still, her tricks charm everybody—including our parental units.

Anna only dates boys from Eppingworth, which is the boys' public school just outside Dunton. It's an ancient institution with a sparkling reputation that only accepts boys from families with vaults of money and equal quantities of breeding. Our parents know nothing about this, of course. Neither do theirs, I'm guessing, considering that she's a common state-school girl.

Anna's cover is Marcia. Mum believes that Marcia and Anna spend every Friday night watching cartoons and drinking cocoa in their frilly nighties, and I suspect she also thinks the same of Frannie and me. We all believe what we want to believe, I suppose—it's much easier and less painful in the long run. That's quote number one of the Elemental Good Sense Guide (which is incidentally under copyright). The Elemental Good Sense Guide is made up of basic observations I make about people and life, which I then turn into sayings. I suppose you could say they're like home-made proverbs, except they're a lot more straightforward, user-friendly and realistic. They're like little nuggets of advice or rules to live by, and each one has proven to be really useful. So far my Good Sense Guide consists of about twenty-six quotes, but I add to this list all the time. I plan to become a writer one day, so it's important that I make these observations about people and the world around me early on in life, before old age shrinks my brain to the size of a gnat. Elemental—that's also my nickname, but it's actually more like "Ella Mental". You see: it changes the meaning entirely. My friends call me Ella Mental because they say I'm a bit soft in the head. Yes, my mind not only wanders; sometimes it leaves me completely. But personally I like to think of my behaviour as full-flavoured rather than mental.

Fran and I quickly forget about Anna's tirade and after scoffing down our lunch, we head up to my bedroom. While I dismally contemplate the tragedy that is my wardrobe Frannie lolls on my bed and gazes up at the small luminous paper stars I've glued to the ceiling. When I'm in bed at night in the dark I imagine I'm lying under a star-studded sky somewhere exotic, and I feel free and fearless. Sometimes I burn Sea Breeze incense to add to the effect, but Mum usually moans the next day that my room smells like a brothel. How she would know what a brothel smells like I've yet to discover.

Tonight is only a gathering of Dunton's dumb and dumber crowd, but Toby likes bold colors so I carefully pick out a red top to go with my jeans and before long we're merrily heading in the direction of Frannie's cozy, detached home. I adore going to Frannie's and would swap families with her any day. Frannie is actually Francisca, and her parents are both Portuguese. She's an only child and disgustingly spoilt, but better still is the amazing love and respect her parents have for her and each other. They're so cool; not like Pearl's mum who doesn't care, but not discipline freaks like my parental units either. Frannie's mum insists that I call her Maria, and she's always really nice to me. I wonder how she feels about adoption.

"I hate lying to your mum," I declare suddenly.

"Maybe she won't ask," Frannie says, immediately guessing what I'm on about.

"She always asks; why shouldn't she this time?" I groan.

We find Maria Mendes sitting in front of her

sewing machine making something frilly from peach material. She's a round woman with blue-black hair and kind, dark eyes that are lined from laughter. She stops sewing when we enter the room. "Ah, look who we have here!" she smiles, pursing her lips and pointing at her cheeks. This means that she wants us both to give her a kiss. Her skin is soft and warm and smells of lavender soap and I don't mind putting my lips to her cheek one bit. Frannie always gets really embarrassed and says that she wishes her mother wouldn't insist on making out with her mates, but I would be secretly devastated if Maria didn't insist on her kiss.

"You girls sleeping here tonight?" she asks in her colourful Portuguese accent.

"Uh huh," we grunt in unison and stare sideways to avoid eye contact.

"And are you going out tonight?"

"We're all meeting up at Michael's house," Frannie replies but doesn't submit any details. Here it comes.

"Does your mother know what you're up to?" This question is directed solely at me and I bob my head vigorously. A nodded lie is definitely better than a spoken lie and even though Maria really is too nice to deceive, sometimes you've just got to do what you've got to do. That's another one of my Good Sense Guide quotes—number nine, I think it is. I'm considering adding a Good Sense quote about lying and what makes a lie okay and what makes it seriously out of order, but I need to think this one through first. It's a very fine line. Lately I seem to be spending a lot of time playing hide and seek with the truth, but that's only because other people keep forcing their will on me. The blame really is not all mine.

Before Maria can settle into her role as quiz master, Fran and I grip our bags and scurry upstairs to play music and prepare for the evening. Frannie is tall with olive skin and dark hair, which is very eye-catching. She's a natural beauty, not like Pearl who takes her makeup tips from Coco the Clown. I really don't know why I'm friends with Frannie, come to think of it. So she's sweet, bright, and funny, but if you consider that I look like a Medusa monster standing next to her then she's probably not the wisest choice for a mate. I really should choose less attractive friends in the future.

Michael and his mates are a bit older so none of us wants to arrive alone, that's why we're all meeting up in the park and walking to the party together—except for Pearl, who is meeting us there. Toby is the last to arrive and I'm glad that he looks for me first. We don't need words; we're always happy to see each other.

Two scruffy blokes are sitting sentry on the pavement outside Michael's house, smoking cigarettes and tracking our approach with hairy eyeballs. "Look what just crawled out from under a rock!" the bigger of the two says to his mate. His hair is matted with the early stages of dreadlocks and he appears to fancy himself, although it seems to me that he could do with a bath, with a good dollop of disinfectant thrown in for good measure. Just then Pearl sashays out of nowhere and thankfully saves us from having to respond to the taunt. She's obviously been waiting for us but is doing her best to appear unconcerned in front of these blokes, which means they're probably Michael's friends. No surprise there.

"I'm so glad you guys could make it," she purrs. Tonight Pearl is one cool cat.

"You look fab!" shrieks Frannie, taking in Pearl's sequined jeans, off-the-shoulder blouse and heels. I've heard it said that less is actually more, but then I'm hardly the fashion guru of Dunton so I just keep my jaws clamped.

Head to toe, Pearl is probably the palest person I know. Her hair is as fair and as fine as cotton and sets the tone for the rest of her coloring—it's almost like she was dipped in a bucket of bleach as a baby. But insead of fading out, Pearl always stands out in a crowd. You'll never see her without her makeup and trimmings, and she spends hours on her hair with its feathered ends and long jagged fringe that swoops down to her small pointy nose with its mischievous curl at the tip. She always looks like she's up to something, and usually is.

"Come on," says Pearl, extending a hand to Frannie and me and leading us in the direction of the music. There are about ten or so other people inside: Most are guys but there are a few girls dotted here and there. They all seem to be hanging about doing nothing in particular, except for one girl who's dancing solo in the corner. Her eyes are closed and she's pulsing to the beat and making jerky Vogue movements *à la* Madonna with her arms. I've definitely seen this type of girl before. The Lone Raver: You can't miss her. She's usually had too much of something and is the first to either pass out or throw up. Lord Michael is sprawled on the sofa pulling on a cigarette. He's not the only one and the air is overcast with smoke.

Pearl signals our arrival and Michael emerges from his cloud to invite us out into the back garden. He has a surprise for us, he says. I hook Toby's gaze and he hoists an eyebrow at me knowingly, but doesn't say anything. So off we tramp through the house and out to the pretty garden with its neat flowerbeds, cobblestone path, and small wooden shed and settle in a spot away from Michael's ghoulish mates (because who knows, stupidity may be contagious). I'm really hoping that Pearl will have the presence of mind to talk herself out of any of Michael's nasty suggestions, until they suddenly appear—their arms cluttered with bottles of every shape and color.

"It's party time!" Michael whoops gleefully and begins distributing the alcohol out between his mates. He must have raided his parents' liquor cabinet; there's no way he could have bought all of this. As Michael heads in our direction I nervously consider my reaction. I really don't want to look like a wimp but I'm no booze-guzzler either. Michael thankfully approaches Alfie first, who unsurprisingly accepts a bottle of clear liquid that's probably vodka or something. Tom-Tom is hesitant and blinks at the vodka like there's a good chance it'll bite him.

"You got a beer instead?" he asks evenly. I've seen Tom-Tom drink beer before, but I've never seen him drunk and next to Toby he's my second favorite male in the entire world. He's quiet, calm, really interesting to talk to, and the sort of person who just oozes respect. But Michael ignores him and leans over to Toby instead.

"What you havin', Sport?"

"Cheers mate," Toby squeezes out a smile and casually refuses the extended bottle, patting his sinewy midriff instead. "I'm in training for the World Cup," he jokes, even though he hates to be called "Sport." Michael stares at him for a second or two—considering whether or not to take this further, and then swings his bleary gaze over to me.

"Well then what about you, Ducky?" he slurs.

Ducky? Just who is he calling "Ducky," I rage inwardly. I really don't give a flying fig what Michael thinks of me—but "Ducky"? Ducky is a hefty frump with facial hair, everybody knows that! I've got a good mind to shove the bottle he's offering where it's dark and dangerous, but angrily snatch it from him instead. "Here's to your health, Ducky!" I blurt out without thinking.

Michael sniggers wickedly. "Thadda girl! And there's plenty more where that came from." Pearl is grinning at me like a simpering idiot; she really thinks we're happily socializing with her greasy boyfriend and his catatonic mates.

"I must introduce you to Dave—he's drop dead!" she whispers in Frannie's ear before prancing off behind Michael.

"I think the term is 'brain dead,'" I murmur to Frannie, who starts chuckling. I don't know if I should be flattered or annoyed that Pearl has chosen to introduce Frannie—and not me—to Dave. To be honest, I'd rather chew glass than meet Dave, but I'd like to think that I was at least considered marketable.

"What do you think you're doing, DUCKY?" Toby suddenly hisses like a burst pipe in my ear. I've a good mind to bash him one.

"Carry on and you'll soon find out!" I growl menacingly, going nose to nose with him. "I'm not going to drink it; I just took it to get rid of Michael."

Toby glowers at me until I can feel his hot breath on my face. Finally he tosses me a fierce frown and turns to Tom-Tom and Alfie, who is now swigging from the mouth of the bottle like a suckling lamb—although I don't see his throat moving very much and suspect that he's doing it more for effect. Toby hates alcohol but says that it's not his place to nag his mates. He must mean his blokey mates, but I ignore the bottle beside me and spend the next half hour dissecting life with Frannie.

The party is growing louder and the guy with the dreadlock-excuse-for-a-hairstyle is now poking about in the shed. Michael doesn't seem concerned and I have a hunch that the evening is set for a head-on collision with disaster. My timing is on target. An intense blue-white flame suddenly ignites and illuminates the interior of the shed.

"Rad man!" Dreadlocks hollers at the top of his voice. He's found a can of paraffin and is lighting puddles of the stuff on the shed's concrete floor. After a while he emerges from the shed looking more dazed than usual and gripping a hammer. "Oi, let's get hammered!" he slurs between spasms of laughter, which inspires the rest of the goons to get in on the destruction. One of them finds a drum kit in the shed and slashes the skin with a screwdriver. Dreadlocks howls his approval.

"Uh oh! Let's get out of here," Tom-Tom and

Toby chime simultaneously. As we make our way through the house I scan the writhing party goers for Pearl. She emerges from one of the bedrooms— lurching along like a newborn calf. I grab her hand but her fingers stay limp in mine.

"Come on Pearl, we're leaving!" I instruct, clutching her droopy fingers even tighter.

"Why should I listen to you?" Her words sound smudged, her eyes are bloodshot, and she's tipsy with too much of something, but luckily Frannie has the sense to grab her free arm and together we frogmarch her out the front door and down the road. Tom-Tom, Toby and Alfie are behind us, although I can see that Alf wouldn't mind staying to witness the bedlam.

"Don't even think about it!" I yell back at him. The air around us starts quivering with the blare of sirens: A neighbor must have called the cops. Two police vans suddenly scream past, their flashing lights trailing a colorful blur. Luckily they don't see us.

"I don't want to leave," Pearl blubbers sulkily and twists her hand from mine. "I can't just desert Michael . . . blub blub."

"Oh button it!" Frannie snaps, and tightening her grip hauls Pearl along with determination.

Toby appears beside me and latches his elbow through mine. "That was a close one!"

"She's a disaster magnet," I say wearily, gesturing to Pearl.

"I'm not deaf you know!" she shouts back though rubber lips.

"That was bound to go belly-up," I mumble, more to myself than to Toby. Life used to seem so much smaller and simpler. Each year at secondary school seems to be getting progressively more complicated and the pressure is mounting from every side. Pressure to keep up with my friends, to be accepted and fit in, to do well at school, to dodge my parental units and get on with my sister, to keep my secrets and cope with the challenges I don't feel strong or brave enough to tackle.

"Well don't get morbid about it!" Toby smiles and puts his arm around my shoulders. There's nothing like a Toby-cuddle to dilute my dark thoughts.

DISCARD

Peabody Public Library
Columbia City, IN

Chapter 3
Sliding Into Second

Anna thinks I'm a scruffy, uninteresting swot. She's embarrassed to admit that we're twins and the fact that we practically have duplicate DNA structures is a scientific mystery to Anna and her snooty mate. She used to encourage me to "try and look a little less like a reject" (her words, not mine), and I did try. Honest. Until I almost poked my eye out with the mascara brush and an unimpressed Toby called me "Anna's lab experiment." So as twins go we could not be more different, although we do love each other really and share a sisterly bond. It may be a hazy bond at times, but it's there—hanging about somewhere. We haven't even looked at each other since our spat over the razor, but I can tell that Anna wants to make up just as much as I do.

"That denim skirt looks cool," I say to her one morning, appealing to her vanity but really meaning it too.

"Thanks," she mumbles, but I can tell she's

grateful that I've broken the skin on our silence. So we walk to school together and chat about the coming Easter break and silly, insignificant things. Anna also tells me about her Eppingworth boyfriend called Spencer Waldron-Worthington. Spencer's dad is a politician, his mum belongs to endless charities, and they breed racehorses and walk on water and zzzzzzzzzz. But her eyes glisten as she talks and she really seems chipper, which makes me like Spencer Waldron-Worthington-Whatever—even if he does have a snobby name.

Then Anna tells me a secret: She's not really going away with Marcia and her parents for the Easter weekend, like she told Mum. She's really sneaking away with Spencer to their family beach house in Devon. I ask her how his parental units feel about this, and she tells me that Spencer and his older brother are allowed to bring friends and anyway, his units are so busy gadding about the place they wouldn't notice if she had three heads. I'm really happy that she's happy, but I wonder what this Spencer might be expecting from my sister. It's a well-documented fact that teenage blokes are walking hormones with one thing on their minds. Not that I would know, of course—no bloke has walked his hormones in my direction—but that's what I've heard anyway. The closest I've come to a relationship with the opposite sex is playing house with Toby when we were kids. He was a very good husband.

"You haven't...you know, done anything, have you?" I ask.

"No, of course not!" she sizzles. "What do you take me for?" Silence.

"But . . . ?" I ask, sensing that there's more she wants to add.

"But . . . I think he may be the one." She says "the one" like she's having a religious experience or something. "He's so wonderful and amazing and I can't imagine ever loving anybody more. We were meant to be together!" she drools.

I can't believe what I'm hearing. Not only is Spencer her first proper boyfriend, but they haven't even been together that long! "So how long have you been dating?" I ask, trying not to make it sound like an accusation.

"About two months," she announces triumphantly.

I don't know whether to be upset or relieved that she's kept all this from me, and we continue walking in silence for a while. Anna may be the older twin but I somehow still feel like the responsible one, which bugs me a bit. *She* should be the one giving *me* advice. I really should get a life—then maybe everybody would stop bothering me with theirs.

"Look, Anna," I say, unable to resist the urge to butt in. "I'm glad you're happy, but take it easy. Just because something feels right at this moment in time doesn't mean it'll feel right for ever." I sound really calm and sophisticated and decide to keep going while I'm still making sense. "And you really have no other boyfriends to compare Spencer to. Men are a lot like Ben & Jerry's ice cream, you know. I mean, what are the chances of you finding your favorite flavor first time around? Look at me: I used to be hooked on Butter Pecan, but now I can't get enough of Peace of Cake. It's called making an informed decision," I finally conclude. I really am good at this.

Anna has come to a complete standstill and is staring at me as if I've just sprouted horns. "You're comparing my love life to frozen dessert?" she bleats indignantly, furious that I've dared to give her relationship advice.

"So I read it in *CosmoGIRL!*" I admit. "Well, except the bit about blokes being like Ben & Jerry's. But the rest comes from a real agony aunt who's had loads of relationships and knows exactly what she's talking about. So just take my, er . . . her advice." This sisterly chat is derailing quickly. With all this advice I'm dishing out you'd think I had no problems of my own.

"You and Toby haven't cornered the market on soul mates, you know!" Anna declares finally and flounces off nose-in-the-air without even a goodbye. What's that about? I wonder, as I traipse in the direction of my form room and friends.

Frannie's been behaving really strangely lately. I think she may be angry with me because lately she doesn't seem to be interested in talking to me or doing anything together. I can't imagine what I've done to upset her, but I've got a secret under my skin and after a few days of festering I finally decide to approach Toby with the news of my sister's dastardly weekend in Devon instead. He's usually not very good at heart-to-hearts—he calls it prattling. Typical bloke, they think a grunt and a wink equals a deep and meaningful conversation, but busybodies can't be choosers and so I stop off at his house after school anyway.

"Hey, Ellie," he says, glancing up from the television in his bedroom.

"Hey, Tobes. What are you watching?" I ask.

"Cartoons, but don't tell anyone. It would ruin my tough-guy image."

"What tough-guy image?" I tease him. "Everyone thinks you're a ninny. That's why I'm friendly with you, because I feel sorry for you. Didn't you know?"

Suddenly Toby grabs me, launches me on to his bed and starts tickling me and tugging my hair until I'm screeching with laughter. I hate being tickled because I can't breathe and end up with hiccups for hours afterwards. That or I end up farting—which is like the most embarrassing thing ever, but Toby has been doing this since we were eight years old and I reckon we'll still be doing it when we're eighty and senile.

"Stop! Stop!" I yell, trying to fight back and kick him off with my legs. I may be smaller but I'm quite strong and he has to work hard to keep me pinned down. The tickling quickly turns to play fighting and I'm ready to bite if I need to. That's the advantage of being a girl: You can get away with biting. If a boy bites then you know he's a nancy boy.

Toby changes tactics and now attempts to reach my clenched armpits (my tickliest bits), but mistakenly squeezes my left breasticle instead! We both freeze up and instantly want to die. Breasticles are entirely new to this game; one day I was happily flat chested and the next day I had these pointy things. Or maybe they were growing all along and I just wasn't paying attention, but either way—they're proving to be rather inconvenient.

"Er . . . sorry Ellie." Toby's come down with split-second sunburn.

"Yeah well, next time keep your grubby mitts off what you can't afford," I huff, mentally praying for Scotty to beam me up to some far-off planet. Any one will do, I'm not fussy.

Toby springs to the floor and we both straighten ourselves out and try to think about something other than my budding chest. I guess you could say that there's chemistry between Toby and me, but not in a boy-girl, penis-vagina kind of way—rather as one human being to another. I think that in a previous life we may even have been related to one another, although some people struggle to understand this concept. But Toby just laughs. He's too preoccupied with football to think much about girls in that sort of way, and I'm . . . well, just too busy coping with this thing called life.

But just because Toby isn't interested doesn't mean the entire female population of Dunton Secondary don't do anything and everything in their power to snag his attention. He's had so many girls batting their eyelids at him he thinks that females were biologically designed to blink twice as much as blokes. Luckily I explained to him that this is what happens when you have a brain the size of a jellybean: Your eyelids get top heavy and you're forced to blink twice as hard to keep them open. I told him in no uncertain terms that he would be very wise to avoid these types of girls. Toby says I have a quirky sense of humour and make him laugh, although I'm usually not trying to be funny. Most of the time I'm being super serious, but I've learnt to just go along with it and laugh when he laughs. I believe that in this life you've got to take what you can get and run with it, because that may be just about all you're getting. That's number two on the Elemental Good Sense Guide.

Now is the perfect time to change the subject and tell Toby about Anna's devious plans. While I dramatically re-enact the story he sits there quietly, nodding every few moments until finally I'm done.

"Mmmm . . . so young Anna Watson is thinking of doing the deed," he chortles wickedly.

"No she's not!" I yelp. "Well, not necessarily like for definite anyway." I should probably have left that bit out; I am now guilty of blabbing both of Anna's secrets. She'd torture me if she knew. "Please Toby, you have to promise to never-ever-ever tell a single soul. Promise?"

Toby holds his head high and strokes his jaw theatrically, and for a moment he looks like he belongs in a boy band. "Yeah, okay," he eventually agrees, completely unaware of my scrutiny.

"Yeah, okay what?" I ask suspiciously. I want to hear his promise in full.

"I promise not to tell a single soul that Anna is planning on shaking her groove thang. . . ."

"TOBY!" I shout.

"Okay, chill! I promise not to tell anyone that Anna is going away with Spencer Wally-Waldron-Worthington the twenty-second. There, happy?"

It's about the best I'm going to get out of him so I nod in agreement. "So what should I do?" I whine.

"There's nothing you can do," he replies. "She's a big girl and she'll make her own decisions, no matter what you think or say. Now I'm going to have a kick-about, do you want to come along?" Toby asks, bouncing his soccer ball carelessly.

I'm beginning to realize that guys and girls really are contrary creatures indeed and that the only thing males are good at is changing the subject. How can we think so differently and yet still be expected to share Earth?

"No, I definitely do not!" I answer, irked by his lack of answers on the Anna situation.

"Suit yourself, but you really should get some exercise," he chimes and disappears down the stairs and out the front door.

What is that supposed to mean? So what if lately I have to wriggle about like a dying cockroach just to get my jeans on? I don't want to play stupid football (oh yawn!) and that's the end of it. I don't want to sit here on my own either and I exit Toby's room in a full-blown huff, but I'm not watching where I'm going and collide with Daftcow Melanie—Toby's older sister, who is slithering across the landing. Melanie is seventeen and one of the slimiest snakes I've ever met. She can't stand to see Toby happy and hates it when she's not the center of the universe. Of course she can be dangerously syrupy when she wants something, but generally speaking she's a conniving, nasty, daft cow.

"Ooops! Oh, hi Ella," she grins ever so sweetly.

Deafening alarm bells! Why is she being nice? "Uh, sorry Daft . . . er . . . Melanie—I didn't see you. How are you?" I ask politely.

"Absolutely eff-ay-bee!" she shrieks, and immediately starts telling me about her brand new job and how the boss has the hots for her blahblahblah, but I'm not listening to her babble.

"I've got to get going," I mutter and stampede down the stairs and out the front door. I'd rather touch dog poo than hear about Melanie and her pervy boss.

Chapter 4
The Devil and the Bright Blue Sea

Just when I finally decide to approach Frannie and ask her why she's being so off to me she suddenly perks up and is her usual friendly self once again. It looks as though she's forgiven me for whatever it is I did or didn't do, and although I'd really like to know what that was, I don't want to risk rowing with my friend. It's lunchtime and chucking buckets so we're trapped in the classroom like prisoners of war. Toby is about to fidget himself right off his chair, Tom-Tom is rocking on his and blowing enormous pink bubbles, Frannie is filing her nails and nattering away, Pearl is no doubt fagging it up somewhere, and I'm staring out at the shards of relentless rain shattering against the window. I have a headache from breathing stuffy, second-hand air.

"Oi, space girl!" a voice barks, crashing my train of thought. How many times must I tell people to stop calling me that? I glance around, searching for the voice. It belongs to Frannie, who appears to be waiting for me to reply to something.

"Huh?" I mumble. I was so not concentrating.

Frannie sighs dramatically. "Are you going to the school social?"

"Erm, well the parental units have actually given us their royal blessing, so I guess so." By us I mean Anna and me, and yes, we're actually allowed to go to the school social tomorrow night, although I haven't discussed it with Toby yet. I'll only go if he goes, of course. And we still have the earliest curfew in England, but it's a start and one less lie on my conscience.

"If there's a party you know I am so there!" a voice booms from behind me. It's Pearl and she's grinning like she just won the lottery.

"Hey Pearl, I hear that little party got your boyfriend Michael in some serious trouble," chants Tom-Tom.

"Yeah," adds Toby, grinning like a Cheshire Cat, "word is that he and his mates are being charged for the damage they caused. One helluva party, huh!"

"For your information we broke up," Pearl declares smartly. "Or to be more precise—I dumped him; although that's not the story he's giving out."

Just then the bell rings and Mrs. Bullock enters the classroom clutching Geography textbooks to her bony bird-chest. Mrs. Bullock is also the deputy head of Dunton Secondary and has been around since dodos skipped the planet, but nobody likes her one bit. Our headmaster is Mr. Povey, although we call him our "dead master" because he's so laid back. He's cool for a teacher, but Mrs. Bullock's life ambition is to get as many kids into trouble as possible. Her nickname is Mrs. Bollocks, and I'm terrified that one day I'll call her this to her face without thinking. That's just the sort of thing I'd do.

We don't acknowledge her and she doesn't bother greeting us. Instead, she immediately launches into her prepared lesson on the rain cycle, taking some small pleasure in the fact that she knows what she's talking about and we've still got to figure it all out. I tear a small square from my foolscap pad, write the words: "U wanna go 2 the social?" on it and fake-yawn-pass it back to Toby—who sits directly behind me, making sure that Bollocks is writing on the blackboard as I do so. I feel a nudge at my hip a few moments later.

I already know that it's Toby's shoe and that the tear of paper will be rolled up and tied in its lace. With eyes face-front I tug at the note and unfold it under my desk.

"I'll go if you go," it reads.

I draw a smiley face on the top of my hand and pretend to scratch my head so that Toby can see it. Party time!

Why does time slow to a dull ache when you're waiting for something exciting to happen? Today has been the longest day ever, but finally school ends and the social beckons. The socials always have a theme and even though it's supposed to be a huge secret, everyone knows that it's "Underwater World." It seems the dance committee doesn't have the budget or the brain matter to come up with anything more original, and so it's always "Underwater World." Non-Dunton pupils are strictly forbidden so Anna's not looking forward to it as much as I am, but tomorrow she leaves for her weekend away so I'm sure she'll find the strength to cope.

Toby and I are walking to the social together and he's supposed to be waiting for me across the road at six o' clock, but he's late as usual and so

I'm wasting time nervously analysing my reflection in the mirror. I've blow-dried my hair and left it loose for a change, which Anna says looks really swish (that's her new word). And I'm wearing jeans, of course, but I've borrowed Anna's bright pink fitted halter-top, which is quite feminine and pretty and turns my pale cheeks rosy. Well, that's what Anna says anyway.

"Toby's here!" she suddenly announces. Her nose has pressed a powdery triangle on the window pane. "And so is Marcia, are you ready?"

I nod anxiously, giving my mirror image a final once-over. I feel vulnerable with my bare shoulders and back exposed to everyone and their opinion, but it's too late to change now and I trail after Anna and make a desperate dash for the front door—hoping to escape with a mid-air "g'bye" in the direction of our parental units.

"See you girls at ten sharp!" our dad grunts from the sofa.

"Yeah," we both mutter.

"Have fun," I say to Anna, squeezing her at the front gate. Sometimes I really do love her, even if she does smell like she's fallen headfirst into a vat of Aphrodisiac *eau de toilette*. I usually call it her "odor of toilet", but Anna gets peeved when I do so tonight I keep schtum.

Toby's hands are shoved in the pockets of his deep blue denims and he's wearing a black and gray button-up shirt that brings out the turquoise in his eyes. Unfortunately his craggy forehead and tight lips don't seem ready for a party. "Hi, sorry I'm late," he mumbles without even commenting on the glaringly obvious fact that I've taken more care than usual with my appearance.

"No prob," I say cheerily, refusing to be disappointed by his shoddy observational skills. "What's up? You look down."

"Nothing," he sighs. This is not like Toby one bit.

"Come on. What's wrong?"

"It's no biggie," he says, angrily punishing a loose stone in the road with his shoe.

"A problem doesn't always have to be a biggie to count," I say confidently. "What makes a problem important is the fact that it's yours." I'm so sharp, one of these days I'm going to cut myself.

"Let me guess," Toby cracks, "that's Elemental Good Sense Guide number two thousand seven hundred and nine?" Apart from Anna, Toby is the only other person who knows about the Good

Sense Guide—although I should add that he didn't seem that impressed when I explained it to him.

"Ha ha," I scoff, making a mental note to add it to the Good Sense Guide when I get home anyway. I don't know what's got Toby's goat but he's obviously not going to be much fun tonight.

"I said it's nothing, Ellie, but if you must know . . . well, it's just that my dad's been working really long hours lately and having to go out of town quite a bit, which upsets my mum. And they've started fighting about it." He looks really serious.

"Oh," I say unintelligently. I always thought that Toby's parental units were perfect and happy, so I don't have any useful advice on hand. "Well, maybe your dad is just stressed out with work and stuff," I say after a few moments.

"Yeah, that's what I said to my mum but she just rubs my head, sniffles to herself, and tells me not to worry about it—like I was three years old or something," Toby replies.

I try to sound reasonable. "Perhaps they had an argument you don't know about. All parental units argue about dumb things, but they usually get over it. Especially your units, they're as together as folks get."

51

"Yeah, maybe," Toby exhales noisily. I can tell that he doesn't want to talk about this any more, so I change the subject and fill the minutes updating him on Anna's trip with Spencer.

"Well I hope she knows what she's getting herself into," he says simply as we pull up at the school gates.

The parking lot is stuffed with teenagers dressed up to look as dressed down as possible, and there's enough hair gel here tonight to resurface the M25. It doesn't take us long to find our friends, who are loitering about and doing nothing in particular, except for Frannie who is noticeably absent.

"Tonight is my lucky night!" Alfie grins mischievously. He loves the girls and generally has his pick of dates.

Frannie appears out of the nearby loo. "Hello sweeties," she sings. She's wearing a denim skirt and matching jacket and looks so pretty, although I can't help noticing the murky half-moons underlining her eyes. Or perhaps it's just a slippery shadow.

"Shall we go in then?" Toby grumbles. He's definitely not a happy camper this evening.

"Pearl, you fancy a quick fag behind the bicycle shed?" beams Alfie.

"Do I ever, man!" she quips, trying to sound gangster heavy, which really irritates me. So far this evening is not turning out as I had hoped.

"We'll see you fag-ends inside then," Toby says impatiently and heads for the doors.

Before we can go inside we have to give our names to the dance committee members seated behind a trestle table at the entrance.

"I can't believe they're taking a roster!" I whisper to Toby, who just shrugs. He's shutting me out completely and I hate it. When I'm sad I open up and share my feelings with him, but he just lowers the blinds and pretends that nobody's home. Typical guy, I guess. At least I have Frannie-I'm-in-a-good-mood-tonight to talk to, I think as we dodge the first of many paper octopus, anchor, and floating fish decorations. The archway leading into the main hall has been festooned with a layer of shiny blue dangling tinsel streamers, which is supposed to represent a waterfall and the entrance into the Underwater World.

"Hey, an Underwater World theme . . . what an original idea!" jokes Tom-Tom. We find this very funny and laugh too, but it seems not everyone thinks like we do.

"You got a problem with water, Afro Boy?"

sneers John Bennie, who is the school wrestling team captain and resident Dunton jerk and bully. He's surrounded by his three thug mates and they look like they're hunting trouble.

"What's that supposed to mean?" Tom-Tom asks carefully.

"We were just wondering," smirks John Bennie, glancing around at his leering mates, "why you have a problem with water? Maybe they don't use it where your tribe comes from, but here in E-n-g-l-a-n-d us civilized folks like to use it to wash and stuff. Don't we, lads?"

The three monkeys nod in agreement, although judging by the state of them I doubt they know much about the subject. Toby tenses and rolls his hands into white-knuckled fists. This doesn't look good.

"Oi! What's going on here?" It's Mr. Povey and he's noticed the group of snoops gathering around us.

"Er, nothing Mr. Povey," John Bennie smiles, "we were just commenting on tonight's lovely theme." The three monkeys nod again.

Mr. Povey's eyes flit suspiciously between John Bennie and us. "Well get moving, you're holding up the line."

"Sure thing," John Bennie croons, giving Tom-Tom an intimidating wave as he disappears beneath the waterfall.

"What the . . . what was that all about?" Toby eventually demands. The rest of us are gobsmacked into silence.

Tom-Tom shrugs. "They've been hassling me for a coupla weeks," he says. "It's nothing I can't handle."

"But why?" I ask, confused.

Tom-Tom shrugs again. "Seems Bennie's mum has taken up with a black guy and left her wrestler boyfriend, who just happens to be white. And it seems that Bennie doesn't approve . . . but I think it's more of a wrestling than a color thing."

"That's not fair! What's that got to do with you? And what are you going to do about it?" I burble furiously.

"Nothing." Tom-Tom's face is expressionless.

"But you have to do something!" I stutter. Where's the justice?

"Let's forget about it tonight and just try to enjoy ourselves," Frannie sensibly advises, and we all track through the waterfall and into the main hall a.k.a. the Underwater World. The dance floor is still empty as most of the kids are milling about and sizing each other up and drinking Cokes from the stand in the corner. Eventually Alfie turns up, but he's without Pearl—who is chatting to that dipstick Michael outside, it seems.

After a while the music takes over and eager party goers head for the dance floor and start putting on the moves. Anna is among them, and she's laughing and appears to be having a good time. And we all thankfully seem to have forgotten about John Bennie and his thugs for the time being, so this evening may turn out okay after all.

"Hey Alfred, remember me?" a voice tinkles sweetly. It's Maddy Pierce and her friend Rebecca something-or-other. Alf usually loathes being called Alfred, but coming from goldilocks Maddy he suddenly doesn't seem to mind as much. I notice the micro-miniskirt she's wearing and wonder why she bothered with it in the first place. She might as well have stuck a Band-aid around her waist and saved herself the money and trouble.

"This is my best friend Becky; we're so close we're like sisters," she gurgles to Alfie and Toby as if Frannie and I are invisible. I expect Toby to give his usual shrug and ignore them, but tonight the arrival of Pinky and Perky seems to cheer him up no end.

"How's it going, girls?" he says, charming them with a glittering smile.

How's it going, girls? Has he completely short-circuited? Suddenly he's chuckling softly at something Pinky (or is it Perky?) has said and running his hand through his hair while I stand there mesmerized. Now Maddy is giggling with Alf and Becky is chewing on her bottom lip and trying her best to look coy while they all talk about the upcoming footy championship. Becky doesn't have too much to add to the conversation and seems more interested in glowering at me through lowered lashes. I'm doing my best to ignore her until I swear I catch her mouthing the words "bye bye" in my direction.

I turn to Frannie for support only to find that she and Tom-Tom have moved to the vibrating dance floor. Traitors! As Toby and Alfie and the oinker sisters chat amongst themselves I hang about like Norma No-Date trying to look casual and pretend that I'm a part of their conversation.

"Want something to drink?" Toby eventually asks, finally finding a moment to acknowledge the fact that I do actually exist. I shake my head miserably, hoping he'll get the hint, but he doesn't and cuts into the crowd with Alf and those yucky girls in tow. Am I supposed to hang about and wait for their return?

Pearl enters through the waterfall looking dazed and upset. She spies me standing there and straightaway starts bubbling over with tears and snuffles. I think we might have our next Pearlodrama on our hands so I walk over and circle her with my arms.

"What's the matter?" She doesn't say anything and continues sobbing on my bare shoulder until I can feel her warm wet tears slip-sliding down my back. This won't do, and I steer her through the clusters of partying teenagers to a quiet spot at the rear of the hall.

"You were right about Michael," she finally snivels. "I thought he wanted to make up but the rat only wanted to make out!"

"I'm sorry," I say tenderly.

"We were outside and he was all over me. People were staring," she pauses to sniff, "and I told him to stop! So he called me a slapper and ran off laughing with his mates."

The thin string of snot trailing from Pearl's left nostril is bouncing up and down as she talks and making it really difficult for me to concentrate. She spouts a fresh flow of salty tears and I just let her cry, believing that it's better to let your emotions flow out of you instead of bottling them up inside where they can go bad. Good Sense Guide number twenty-three: Always acknowledge your emotions! They serve a purpose and should never be ignored. The only downside of her bawling is that her cheeks are now marbled with streaked mascara.

"Michael was just mean because you're too good for him and he knows it," I say, trying to ignore her Halloween makeup. "Now fix your face and try to forget about him." Pearl considers my suggestion for a few seconds, nods and begins dabbing at her face with a tissue from her handbag. Maybe I should become a psychiatrist instead of a writer.

Just as we're about to head out on to the teeming dance floor, DJ Love-Me-Tender decides to bring the party mood to a grinding standstill with a snog-song. As the speakers ooze with honeyed harmonies the dance floor drains of everyone except the drooling couples, who are now shuffling along and clutching each other as if expecting an earthquake. That's when I spot a familiar face on the dance floor. It's Toby, and his arms are clasped firmly about that beastly Becky's midriff as he sways to the music with his eyes closed! The sight of it makes me feel quite woozy, although I don't really know why it should. I remain motionless, willing myself to turn away but feeling powerless to do so. When I do finally remember how to walk I discover that Pearl has found Tom-Tom and Frannie, or they've found her, but either way—they're all standing together.

"I've got a bit of a headache," I say to everyone and no one in particular.

"But it's only eight-thirty!" complains Frannie. "You're finally allowed out and now you're going home early?"

"I didn't say I was going home," I sigh, although secretly I was thinking about it. But Frannie does have a point.

"Come on, there's someone seriously fanciable I want you to meet," Pearl declares with an impish wink as she connects her arm to mine.

As much as I find Pearl's matchmaking highly amusing, it's only amusing when it doesn't involve me. Someone please just stab me in the heart with a cardboard swordfish and get it over with quickly, I think to myself dismally. This is the first time she's tried to set me up and I'm sure it has something to do with Toby and that girl. My entire universe is out of sync.

But Pearl won't be dissuaded and hastily hauls me off to the other end of the hall while I keep my right eye (the one closest to the dance floor) squeezed tightly shut so that I don't have to see Toby and Beastly Becky dancing together. The downside to this tactic is that when Pearl comes to an abrupt halt I end up rear-ending her painfully.

"Try using your brake lights next time!" I mutter, rubbing my poor mashed nose which is now sticky with Pearl's hair products.

"This is my cousin Glen!" Pearl announces proudly, like she made him herself. I follow her outstretched arm and find myself gazing up at deep dimples, clear skin and gigantic hazel eyes.

"Helloooo, heaven . . . ," I whisper.

"Pardon?" he rumbles.

"I . . . um . . . hi, Glen," I stutter, unable to think of anything quick-witted to impress him with.

"This is my friend Ella," Pearl thankfully comes to my rescue.

"Nice to meet you, Ella," Glen says, a little too casually to be sincere, and sends me a wily wink.

"Yeah, hi," I say again. His stunning smile has jammed my repeat button.

"Glen is new to Dunton, he's just moved here from Eastbourne," Pearl explains, answering the only intelligent question I could think of.

"Cool," I say. I am the queen of small talk. Not!

"But Glen's in Year Eleven," Pearl says.

Right, that's it! I am now officially out of intelligent questions and I haven't even asked a single one yet.

"Cool," I repeat bleakly.

"Yeah, cool," he says, looking at the floor and then at his friends beside him. They soon start talking amongst themselves and Pearl aims her elbow at my ribs.

"Have you watered your brain today?" she hisses in my ear.

"I'm sorry," I say under my breath, "you took me by surprise is all."

"No kidding!" Pearl grunts sulkily.

"We're going to get something to drink, do you want anything?" Glen asks, detonating another wink with his left eye. My face is fixed with a dim-witted smirk and I shake my head politely. Pearl yanks me back on to the dance floor.

"You really are clueless, you know that!" she scolds me over the blare of the music.

"I'm sorry, Pearl, but you know I'm no good with surprises—especially yummy ones!" My face is still petrified into a silly half-grin and for a few moments I forget about Toby and what's-her-face. If only they weren't sitting just a few metres away from me! I can't help glancing in their direction—they must be talking about something really interesting because they appear to be joined at the forehead. My belly does a flip-flop, but I ignore it and for the next few minutes concentrate on looking cool, calm, and in control of my dance moves.

"Where did you girls go to?" a voice unexpectedly gurgles from behind me. I look up and see Glen and his delicious dimples smiling down at me. His teeth are white and perfect and he smells like an advert for aftershave. At least he can dress properly, unlike Becky and the handkerchief she's mistaken for a blouse.

"Uh . . . a good song came on," I lie.

"Mind if we dance with you?" he asks, jerking a thumb at the bloke standing beside him.

"Yeah, sure," I answer casually. Like a girl has ever said no to him! Glen, his no-name friend, Pearl and I form a circle and I'm relieved to find that Glen is quite a good dancer. I usually get stuck with the guy that moves like a frog in a blender. I'm also relieved that the music is too loud for small talk; I sound much more intelligent when I keep my mouth shut. I do, however, wish that Glen would stop with the cheesy winking. Every time he looks my way he snaps me another one and I'm beginning to wonder if he has something in his eye.

After a while the music fades and the DJ's voice echoes over the loudspeakers. "That's it for tonight, guys and dolls," he croons, "but I'm playing out with one last ballad for the lovebirds!"

"Would you like to dance?" Glen's voice drips with schmooze like he's done this countless times before (which he probably has).

"Uh . . . okay sure," I stutter, sounding like I've never done this before (which I haven't). It seems that Toby's not the only one with a ticket for a cruise on the love boat.

Glen folds his brawny arms around my waist and pulls me closer, and I have the sense to copy the girls around me and lock my hands behind his neck. His scrumptious smell fills my nostrils and flows up my nasal passages, into my bloodstream and through to my brain, which makes the room spin a bit, so I close my eyes and concentrate on remaining upright.

"I thought you didn't like me," he whispers in my ear, hot-wiring a shiver that travels along the length of my spine and erupts in a thousand goosebumps on my neck.

"Er . . . what made you think that?" I ask nervously.

"Well, you just disappeared on me, for starters," he grins.

"You went to get a drink," I answer. Was he expecting me to hang about on the off chance that he might return? What is it with these males?

"Anyway, it doesn't matter. At least we're having the last dance together," he says softly, which makes my neck do the goosebump thing again. Glen may be arrogant and fancy himself a bit too much, but he's definitely eye candy with extra toppings.

We dance close together and I'm oblivious to the hoards of hormone-fuelled teenagers lurching around us. But the song and the evening must end and when it does the room explodes with the bright white glare of the overhead fluorescent lights. This must be Bollocks' contribution to the evening.

Just as I'm about to reclaim control of my

runaway senses Glen takes my chin in his right hand and lifts my mouth to his. His lips are squashy and warm and his other arm winds firmly around my neck, and I feel helpless wallowing in his sturdy embrace. I'm just starting to get comfortable when all of a sudden I feel his soggy tongue shove its way into my mouth! This is an entirely new sensation for me and although I think I might grow to like it in time, right here right now it just feels wrong. Perhaps it's because I didn't even know that he existed until a few hours ago; maybe it's the glaring overhead fluorescent lights; or maybe it's because I'm just a dunderhead drag—but my impulse is to turn my head sideways and break free from his clutch.

"What's the matter?" Glen asks, looking baffled.

"Nothing . . . nothing at all," I say, feeling just a tad humiliated. "It's just extremely bright in here, isn't it?"

Glen cases the room. "Yeah, maybe you're right. Let's go outside."

I can't explain why, but I don't want to go outside with him or kiss him any more. "I have to go," I say, shaking my head and heading for my friends. Toby is there and my gaze runs into his, but his eyes are flat and empty. I suppose he must have seen me kissing Glen. The floor was fairly empty at the time so it would have been rather difficult to miss the event. Who knows, maybe he was kissing Becky Hoochie Mama at the same time, but I don't want to think about this now and I say my goodbyes and head off home alone. I need to autopsy the evening in my head. I've just lost my snogging virginity (big secret) to a seriously gorgeous bloke, which means I should be bouncing about on Cloud Nine. So why am I stuck on Cloud big fat Zero?

Chapter 5
Telling Tall Tales

When I wake up the next morning, Anna has already left for her weekend away with Spencer. Pity, I would have liked the chance to say goodbye. Looking out of my bedroom window I notice that Dad is repainting the wooden fence at the back of our garden, which means that I'll also be repainting the fence at the back of the garden. In fact, I'm surprised he hasn't woken me already. Dad can be a bit jolly-hockey-sticks when it comes to delegating chores; I think he sees it as some bizarre family bonding ritual, and I wouldn't mind it as much if he didn't make it such a miserable experience. He's never satisfied and we always end up squabbling furiously until Mum takes his side and I get the silent treatment. I'm throwing myself a leaving party when I finally get out of here.

My howling hunger drags me downstairs. As I stagger into the kitchen Mum explodes through the back door. Her hair is tangled and her face has the pale polished look of somebody who's been rushing about madly. You'd think that a woman of her age would start taking it a bit easy.

"So where's Anna really gone then?" she gasps, her voice rising with just a smidgen of panic. She could beat around the bush a bit first, at least.

"What do you mean?" I croak. My hammering heart is about to hop its way right out of my gaping mouth. I need a minute to think! "Oh, and I'm fine thanks."

"I think you know exactly what I mean," she answers tightly, completely ignoring my sarcastic play for time.

"I'm quite sure I don't," I say, trying my best to sound bored.

"Ella, I've just bumped into Marcia's mum at the grocers. I stupidly thought that maybe they just hadn't left for their trip yet, but when I mentioned it she didn't seem to know what I was talking about! Not only are they not going away—but they're not expecting Anna for the weekend either!" What started off as a normal sentence has now ended in a shrill shriek; any louder and Dad will hear, and then Anna's in for it.

"Maybe you misunderstood Anna? Maybe it's

not Marcia she's gone away with?" I suggest, feeling myself sinking deeper and deeper into the quicksand of Anna's deceit. I think it's really unfair that I'm being dragged into this and forced to rat out my twin sister—and to our miserable parental units, of all people! That's just fundamentally wrong. The irony of the situation is that Anna is probably still only down the road and hasn't theoretically done anything wrong yet. But you can be sure that she's going to be in the steamiest pile of dung for it when she does.

"Ella, I'm not a CENSORED idiot!" roars Mum, adding a rather indecent swearword before the word "idiot."

"Nice language," I comment flippantly. "What sort of example is that you're setting?"

I am so doing the tango with Death. Mum raises her hand as if to slap me but stops herself mid-air, only centimeters away from my face. Her eyes are on fire and I can see that she's using every ounce of her strength to rein in her temper.

"Ella, now try getting this into your thick skull," she speaks slowly and carefully as if she's conversing with a moron. "Anna could get herself into all sorts of trouble!"

Like that's news, I think to myself. Mum

waits for her words to take effect, but I remain where I am and simply stare at her defiantly. The funny thing is that I do understand where she's coming from and why she's upset. I really do. But what I've never understood about my mother is how she can expect me to respect her when she doesn't show *me* the slightest bit of respect. If I had sworn at her I would have been slapped from here to the next millennium, but it's fine for her. And Dad is even worse. You earn respect, you don't demand it: That's Elemental Good Sense Guide quote number fourteen. I remember that it's number fourteen because I came up with it on my fourteenth birthday. But that's another story.

"Look, I don't know anything!" I lie like a convict. "I'm not Anna's keeper. And like I said—maybe you've got the wrong friend. You're the parent here, not me!"

I continue to glower at her rebelliously and even though I know I'm probably doing the wrong thing by lying, I simply can't help myself. I'm not doing my mum any favors after the way she just treated me—especially if it involves snitching on Anna. Case closed. So lucky me: I now have three entire days in which to bear the brunt of my parental units' anger towards my swindling sister.

My appetite seems to have disappeared along with Anna's luck and I trudge upstairs to my bedroom and contemplate trying to call my troublesome twin. I must warn her that she's probably not going to live to see her fifteenth birthday (and should therefore have a blast while she still has a heartbeat), but I'll bet a full tube of Zit-Be-Gone that she'll let her mobile ring to voicemail when she sees it's a call from home. And I don't have any airtime left on my mobile. Toby will let me use his phone, I'm sure of it, but first I'll have to escape this house. And that's not going to happen until I get involved in painting the hateful fence. Sometimes you just have to accept the things you cannot change, otherwise you'll just waste good time and energy trying. I think that somebody has already gone public with that bit of advice, but I'm going to make it Good Sense Guide number twenty-seven regardless.

My diary is my most precious possession and I keep it hidden safely beneath the tissues in the tissue box that stands on my bedside table. Nobody would ever think to look there. My diary is almost full and when it is I think I may write to the editor of *CosmoGIRL!* and tell her about the Elemental Good Sense Guide, so that she can publish it for all the Cosmo Girls to read. I extract my diary from of its cozy nest of two-ply, open it up and add the quote to the Good Sense list. Then I put on some old clothes and drag myself down to the fence.

Luckily, Dad's disappeared (I think he's in conference with Mum), so I finish the painting in supersonic speed and zip over to Toby's without even bothering to change my clothes or clean the splattered paint off my skin. I must warn Anna!

Walking up to Toby's front door I realize that I'm actually nervous to see my best friend. Our friendship has never had to cope with the interference of another guy or girl before and I'm suddenly afraid that it might change things between us. And what if he really fancies Beastly Becky? She's hardly his type, is she? What is his type anyway? I've never seen him act like that before, so how can I be sure? And what if he mentions my Glen-snog? Not that I had much to do with it. I kept my tongue to myself—in my mouth where it belongs—but Toby doesn't know that and it's not exactly something that's easily dropped into the conversation.

Usually I walk straight into Toby's house as if it was my own, but today I feel compelled to ring the doorbell. Toby answers after a minute or so and definitely seems startled to see me.

"Ella Mental . . . ," he snorts.

"Who were you expecting, the Queen?" I snap, annoyed that things appear to be different already. I'm supposed to waft in unannounced and he's supposed to treat me like I'm part of the furniture. This is definitely changing the rules.

"I just figured you'd be out sucking face with lover boy," he drawls sourly.

"I'm surprised you found the time to figure anything out," I bite back, bruised by his comment. "I thought you'd be too busy taking dirty dancing lessons from Becky the bratty . . . beastly . . . whatchama-call-her . . . !"

Toby chooses to ignore the fact that I'm not making much sense and thankfully changes the subject to my appearance. "Ella, I'm not sure if you've noticed, but an enormous bird seems to have pooed all over you. Thank goodness cows can't fly." That's more like it.

"Ha ha. You're funny. It's paint, git!" I reply, dismissing my white splattered clothes and pushing past him into the tidy Sinclair living room. He teases me and I get snotty; that's our routine. Maybe nothing needs to change after all. "Guess what?" I continue, eager to reverse the conversation away from Beastly and Glen. "Mum discovered that Anna hasn't gone away with Marcia! I must call Anna and warn her. Could I use your phone?"

"What's wrong with yours?" Toby asks.

"I don't have any airtime on my mobile and I just know Anna will ignore any calls from home," I reply.

"Yeah, okay," he says, pointing to the cream handset on the hall table.

I press Anna's number and it goes straight to voicemail. Her recorded voice advises me to leave my name as well as the date and time of my call. She then promises to return my call when she can. Oh, she also thanks me for calling. There's a good chance I'll draw my first pension check before I hear the wretched beep. "It's me, Ella," I eventually crow into the mouthpiece, and then reveal how Mum bumped into Marcia's mum at the grocer's and how she's been found out. Now all I can do is hope she retrieves the message soon.

"And?" Toby emerges from the kitchen with a drink in his hand.

"Voicemail," I say, "I left a message."

"I'm watching some James Bond re-run,"

Toby mumbles as he wanders in the direction of the television room. That's Toby's version of an invitation, which means that things have almost returned to normal again. I want to ask him about Becky, but I know that will mean I'll have to answer questions about Glen and I'm not up for that. I really just want to hang out with my best mate. For once I want to observe the blokey rule of just keeping quiet and pretending that everything is perfect. And so even though we've already watched every 007 movie ever made, I can't think of another thing I would rather be doing.

Chapter 6
Crossing Enemy Lines

The parental units have obviously given up on me and joined forces with Marcia's parental units who have threatened poor Marcia into talking. They now know that Anna is in Devon with Spencer and have contacted his parents who—although haughtily refusing to cut their holiday short, have promised to keep a very close eye on her. "And your son!" Dad was very quick to add. My stupid act seems to have worked; maybe I should forget about becoming a writer or a psychiatrist and join MI6 instead. I obviously have a talent for keeping secrets.

It's Sunday morning and both units are thankfully heading off to who-knows-where, but I don't fancy staying home. I'm impatient to talk to somebody about Glen and our snog and Anna and Beastly Becky, and considering that I haven't seen Frannie since Friday I suppose we're way overdue for some girlie dialogue. When I arrive at the Mendes' home Maria informs me that

Frannie is in her bedroom, which is where she's apparently been all weekend. I make my way upstairs to find the door partly open and Frannie stretched out across her bed, still in her pajamas and watching some talk-show rubbish on telly.

"It's almost twelve o'clock!" I say by way of a greeting. "Why are you still in your jim-jams?"

Frannie lifts her head bleakly from the pillow and gives me a feeble wave. "Hi, Ells. Come in."

"Are you feeling sick?" I ask worriedly.

"Close the door, won't you," she sighs. "Nah, I'm not sick. I just don't feel up to facing the world today."

"But your mum says you've been in bed all weekend," I bleat.

"Are you and my mum in cahoots? Her nagging is about all I can handle, so if you want to hang out—lay off, huh?" And with that Frannie turns and continues watching the telly screen, where a plump girl with bleached white hair and a nose ring is sobbing. Sitting beside her is a guy with scary acne and tacky tattoos, and I can't decide if he's more bored or embarrassed by her blubbering. The words "Is Your Love a Love Rat?" are plastered across the bottom of the screen. I'll bet money that he is.

"So what have you been up to?" I casually ask, hauling my gaze away from the young couple eager to gamble their dignity on half an hour of televised fame and focusing on the dishevelled lump that used to be my primped and perfect friend Frannie instead.

"Nothing much," she sighs. I detect a trace of irritation in her voice, which reminds me that having a conversation with Frannie these days is like juggling steak knives blindfolded. I so badly want to ask her about Toby and you-know-who, but I don't want to sound all me, me, me—so I wait for her to broach the subject.

"You hear about Tom-Tom?" she eventually asks, piercing the bristly silence.

"No. What about him?" I respond.

"John Bennie and his mates followed Tom-Tom to the car park as he was leaving the social on Friday night, and they started pushing him about and stuff," she relates.

"No way!" I choke. Toby didn't mention a word about it so I wonder if he even knows. "What happened?"

"Alfie was with him, and you know what he's like. Tom-Tom warned them to back off before things went too far, but Alfie got fed up with the negotiations and decked John Bennie—cracked him one right across the chops."

Poor Tom-Tom, I think. He really doesn't deserve this bullying. Of course he could strike back if he wanted to, but I wonder how long he'll be able to hold them off before he's forced to stoop to their level.

"Mr. Povey heard their shouting and came to investigate," Frannie adds dully. "Luckily he didn't catch them, but he did break up the fight." She doesn't seem all that interested in the news and her voice carries all the spin and thrill of a weather report. She doesn't mention Glen or our snog or Becky either, but I hang out with her for a while—ever hopeful, until finally she falls asleep on me. Now I realise that I'm not front-page news, but please let me believe that I'm interesting enough to at least keep my friends awake?

The following evening I'm up in my room while the parental units are lying in wait for Anna but pretending to watch some dim-witted sitcom on telly. Thanks to drywalls I can almost hear everything, and when the door finally swings open the first words spoken spill from Mum.

"What were you thinking!" she demands in a

high-pitched screech. She's got to lay off the helium. Then I hear an indistinguishable thudding sound, followed by what can only be our dad's voice.

"For your own sake you'd better get out of my sight!" he bellows. "You've got a lot of explaining to do, but right now I don't even want to look at you!" This means that he's too angry to talk, which—if you happen to be standing in Anna's boots—is not all bad. Yes, he may be backbreakingly furious, but at least he's having the sense to wait until he's cooled down a bit. You definitely do not want to wrangle with our dad when he's lost the plot.

I can hear the units talking to somebody at the door and I guess it must be the Waldron-Worthingtons. The next thing I hear is Anna plodding up the stairs and entering her room, and after a few minutes of silence I risk going to see her, tapping on her door lightly and entering without waiting for her permission. Normally this would be suicidal, but tonight's situation is slightly out of the ordinary. I expect to find her crying and morbid, but instead I'm greeted by a cocky and rather nonchalant Anna. Her left cheek is scarlet, and she's rubbing it gingerly.

"I suppose I should've expected a slap,

shouldn't I?" she says. Her eyes are big and bright and gleaming and it looks as though she's ready to take on the world.

"Did you get my message?" I ask, worried.

"Oh yeah, ta for that! But the game was up and the damage done so I just tried to enjoy my weekend with Spence," she answers with a mad grin stretching her lips.

Ta for that? Could whoever stole my sister please put her back where you found her? "Well the least you could've done was call and let me know that you'd received my message! I've been sitting here stewing, worried that you'd arrive home armed with some ready-made lies!" I snarl angrily, feeling annoyed and hurt at the same time. It's so typical of Anna not to think further than her own nose. "I wouldn't like to be in your shoes right now," I grumble. Actually she's wearing a rather nice pair of suede boots, but that's not what I mean. The old Anna would have been a snivelling wreck in this situation, and I find her newfound bravery startling.

"So how was the weekend?" I eventually ask the alien who's standing in for my sister.

"Swish!" She gives a lazy smile. "But I'm desperate for a bath and bed. I presume I'm grounded so I've got plenty of time to unpack tomorrow." She stands there staring at me expectantly, and after a few moments I twig that she wants me to leave her room. So much for a sisterly chat!

Is no one in this world interested in hearing about my snog or the fact that my best friend may have a new best friend? That's it—I'm never ever showing interest in anybody else's problems ever again, especially not Anna's or Frannie's. I return to my room with the certainty that tomorrow the Watson household will be brimming with tension; we do not deal with conflict well. And what dear, irresponsible, lovesick Anna doesn't realize is that she's making my life a misery too. Just as I was getting used to yesterday, along came today. And now there's tomorrow to worry about. I can't wait to go back to school. How naff is that?

Chapter 7
Spilt Beans

Frannie, Pearl, the boys, and I usually meet in the school quad and spend our lunch breaks together and today it's no different, although for a change it's really nice out. The once-bare trees have perked up a bit and are speckled with miniature buds that are ripe and ready to rupture into shiny new leaves. Spring has almost sprung and the fever is catching. Even Frannie is beaming like a girl in love and judging by the exuberant way she greets me, you'd almost think it was me she was in love with. I really can't keep up with this girl. Pearl arrives next and straightaway grins at me. Finally someone acknowledges my snog, I think uneasily. I had hoped this would go a different route.

"So how's Glenny-poohs?" she coos. I'm not convinced that this is the time or place to go into a full-scale discussion on the matter, but beggars can't be choosers. And it's important that Toby hears how I really feel, so I speak very loudly.

"Actually, I have to admit that I'm not sure I fancy him. I mean, I know that he's fit and I realize he's your cousin, Pearl—but, well . . . I just don't know," I dither, hoping she can help me make sense of it all. A dark cloud moves over Pearl's face and for an instant she appears dangerously irked, although the menacing shadow passes again so quickly I'm left wondering if I imagined it. Still, I somehow don't think this was the answer she wanted to hear.

"And how about you, Romeo?" she turns and gushes cheerily, dangling an arm around Toby's neck. "Have you met the babe of your dreams?" Her attitude deflates me and I sit there pondering the mystery that is my friendship with Pearl.

"If I did, do you think I'd share it with you lot?" Toby quips in between mouthfuls of hotdog.

"You should be asking if he's met the football of his dreams," giggles Frannie, unaware of the tense undercurrent that's surging between Pearl and me.

"What happened between you and John Bennie?" I ask Tom-Tom, changing the subject rapidly. If anybody mentions Beastly Becky's name I think I'll lay an egg.

"Oh, nothing worth talking about," grunts

Tom-Tom, concentrating on carefully picking the cucumber slices out of his sandwich. He doesn't appear too fazed by Friday night's little show-down.

"Show them the text message!" orders Frannie.

"Nah," sighs Tom-Tom. He hates the limelight.

"What text message?" Toby, Pearl and I chime in unison.

"Go on!" urges Frannie.

"Well . . . okay then," Tom-Tom heaves, although it seems he's agreeing simply because it's easier than arguing with Frannie. He retrieves his mobile from his blazer pocket, presses a few buttons and begins scrolling down the screen, reading as he goes along.

```
U DO NOT BLONG HERE HALF-BREAD. THIS IZNT A
RUBBISH DUMP. WE DO NOT WANT YR KIND
OF TRASH HERE SO GO BACK 2 THE JUNGLE.
```

"Except the idiot can't spell 'breed' and has called me a 'half-bread' instead. A half bread! Ha ha." Tom-Tom's laughter sounds dry and forced.

"You should show that to Mr. Povey," I cry out angrily.

"The message just comes up as a 'no number,' so what good would it do me? I can't prove anything," Tom-Tom answers. "Anyway, I'm not a tattle-tale. Nah, it's cool—I can handle it."

"But this isn't the first message he's received," adds Frannie, sounding just a bit like a game show host.

"There must be something you can do mate," Toby says seriously.

"I should give him a good hiding, but that just brings about a whole new set of troubles, doesn't it? No, I'll have to handle it another way," states Tom-Tom.

Just as I'm about to add that he shouldn't have to handle it at all, who should amble by but Pearl's cousin Glen! For someone who is new to the school he appears to be very cocksure and confident, and Pearl gives him an animated wave in greeting.

"Heeeey Glen!" she bays across the quad so that everyone from here to Guatemala can hear her. "You do know that Ella Mental Watson fancies the pants off you, don't you!"

She jabs her finger in my direction—just in case he should miss the burning beacon that is now my blood-red face. I fear I may die of embarrassment. In fact, I would gladly die of embarrassment, because that would be far better than the mortifying humiliation I'm experiencing at this very moment. Glen seems to love the attention, however, and he grins at me and dishes out a wink before heading off with his mates. Right now I'd give anything to have somewhere to hide my head, and for a few brief seconds I hate Pearl and her cheesy cousin passionately. And since when did winking become cool, anyway? From this moment on Glen will forever be known as "Cyclops." Cyclops the winking, one-eyed monster.

"What are you like?" I glower at Pearl.

"I saw you dancing with him on Friday night," sings Frannie.

"Dancing!" cackles Pearl. "They practically sucked the face right off each other! I almost had to dial 999!"

"I think you're exaggerating just a bit," I warble nervously. I can feel my tear ducts grinding into action. "And anyway Pearl, I just told you that I don't really like—"

But before I can finish Pearl cuts me off mid-sentence and starts telling everyone about some saucy graffiti she saw written on the walls of the girls' changing room.

I'm getting really fed up with her tap dancing on my feelings. "Pearl Munroe, the only sport you play is tonsil hockey so I can't imagine what you'd be doing in the girls' changing room in the first place!" I bark at her.

Pearl is flabbergasted by my retaliation. Her smug grin has melted and for the first time her big fat mouth remains unmoving, which is a very satisfying vision. I wouldn't normally challenge Pearl and I wish I had the guts to tell her to hop on her bike and follow the signs to hell, but this is the best I can manage. All the other girls listen to what Pearl says. Not because they particularly like her, but because she's the sort of person you're better off being on friendly terms with. I'm a gigantic baby and as threatening as a stuffed toy on Valium. Good Sense Guide number fifteen: Friendship is a dual carriageway—it runs both ways. Selfish people take without giving back and drain your energy, so learn to spot them and you'll save yourself a lot of time and trouble, because they usually don't change. I really must start screening my friends in future.

The end-of-lunch bell sounds and the quad groans and stands up in one synchronised movement.

"Are you coming to my place after school?" Toby asks.

I usually spend most afternoons at Toby's house so I'm very relieved that Cyclops and his fag-stinker cousin haven't ruined everything. And now Toby knows that I don't fancy Glen. That's the most important thing in the world to me. "Yes, I guess so," I answer quietly.

Chapter 8
Matters of the Heart

From the outside there's nothing particularly special or unusual about Toby's house; most houses in England look similar, although some are better cared for than others. But Toby's house has always been like a second home to me—sometimes more like a home than my own home, and for this reason it stands out from the rest of the brown, pebble-dashed, semi-detached houses that line the streets of Dunton. Toby's mum is home and perched at the kitchen table staring at a piece of paper in her hand. Her head is somewhere else and she lurches with fright when she realizes that we're standing in the kitchen beside her.

"Hey guys," she stammers. Her eyes are red and blotchy as if she's been crying.

"What's wrong?" Toby asks, his voice trembling with apprehension and concern.

"Nothing much," she breezes, rapidly dabbing at the damp skin around her eyes with her sleeve. "My hay fever is back, that's all."

Even I can tell that she made that up on the spot and I feel embarrassed to be intruding on what has the potential to be a serious mother-son moment. "Er . . . excuse me Mrs. T, I'm off to the loo," I mumble. I always call Toby's mum "Mrs. T." When I was a little kid I used to call her Mrs. Toby, which was rather cute—I thought. But now that I'm five foot tall with blossoming breasticles and a tank full of hormones I think "Mrs. T" is a suitable compromise.

"You do what you like, Ella—I'm off to lie down for a bit," she replies, getting up from her chair and folding the paper in her hands. "Toby, your dad's going away for a couple of days, but I'm sure he'll give you a call and chat to you about it himself." And with that she does an about-turn and heads upstairs, taking the opportunity for any further interrogation with her.

"Right!" snorts Toby with an expression that falls somewhere between angry and fearful.

"What's going on?" I ask tentatively.

"Don't I wish someone would tell me!" Toby bellows loud enough for his mum to hear. "My dad is hardly ever here any more and when he is they're always arguing, and my mum walks around with red eyes telling me not to worry myself because everything is all right. But everything is obviously not all right! I just wish they would come out with it and tell me what's going on!"

I've never seen Toby this upset before and I'm uncertain how to navigate this uncharted territory. "Come on, let's head up to your room," I suggest, stalling for time.

Toby's room is rather plain, and apart from the football posters and gleaming trophies lining the single shelf on the wall, it's almost impersonal. I guess that he's just the outdoorsy type and couldn't be bothered decorating a room he doesn't spend very much time in. Or maybe decorating bedrooms is more of a girlie thing? When Toby was younger he had an entire vintage car theme going in this room. The wallpaper and curtains were printed with pictures of miniature Model T Fords in various shades of brown and cream and the shelf was cluttered with old Matchbox cars that had steering wheels that turned and doors that really opened. But the vintage car decor was turfed out with Toby's Lego set and since then the walls have remained white and the linen an everyday shade of blue. I really miss those little cars.

I abandon my bag at the door and grab Toby's

enormous blue continental pillow off the bed and plop it down on the floor in front of the CD player. Toby and I often lie on either side of the pillow, with our heads resting ear to ear and our chins and bodies facing in opposite directions. Sometimes we lie there and chat, other times we just listen to music. But either way, it's a tradition and at this moment in time I think Toby needs some tried and tested familiarity. He chooses a CD and we both settle down to listen to our thoughts and the music. I know that Toby will talk when he's ready.

"Ellie, I haven't told anyone this, but I think my folks are going to get divorced," he finally reveals.

The news shocks me speechless. Not the Sinclairs; how can that be? "You can't be serious!" I squawk tactlessly. "I mean—what makes you think that?"

"Things . . . ," Toby shrugs, "arguments."

"Everybody argues, Toby. It doesn't mean divorce. And anyway, it's like you're always telling me: Don't worry about things until they happen—especially if you have no control over them in the first place." Unfortunately this is the best I can come up with without prior notice, but at least the advice is relevant. Come to think of it, it's a rather good piece of advice to give to anybody and should probably be included in the Good Sense Guide.

"I don't want to be one of those kids who's shoved between one parent and the other," Toby continues, ignoring my advice completely. "In the beginning both parents fight over you, and then eventually neither of them wants you because they're too busy enjoying their freedom and new lives. I don't think I could stomach watching my parents being single and behaving like frisky teenagers again. I don't want my dad to start working out or see my mum with a makeover, because that's what divorced people do, you know—they get makeovers and join gyms and stuff. I like things the way they are. I like my parents the way they are. I don't want to be introduced to my dad's girlfriends or meet my mum's boyfriends, or hear about how they'll always be my friend as well as my parent. Barf! Tell me, why should my life be turned upside down just because they can't keep it together?"

I lie there for a while—with my head beside Toby's—tasting his words. "That may all be true, but you don't want your parents to be miserable, do you?" I ask. "Isn't it better to deal with their divorce and get it over with than spend the next few years living in an unhappy, angry home?" Even though I know I have a point, I still can't help feeling that I'm somehow downgrading Toby's claim to happiness and offering him the consolation prize instead. "You've got every right to feel the way you do, but what if things are not as they seem?" I add, reaching behind me to ruffle his thick blond hair reassuringly.

"I'm just so terrified of losing the people I care about," Toby says softly, putting his hand over mine. He remains quiet and I sense him turn his head and reposition his body so that he's lying on his side and resting on one elbow. But I don't move. Then, as if in slow motion and without saying a word, he folds his hand around the curve of my cheek and gently brings his upside-down mouth to mine. My eyes close and the instant our lips touch my head fills with a thousand fireflies that suddenly sparkle and sizzle and spin around and around like a Catherine wheel. His mouth tastes of marshmallows and his lips are softer than I could ever have imagined. My senses are completely overrun by the extreme closeness of my best friend, who all of a sudden smells and sounds and feels so very different. There's a peculiar electric energy coursing through my veins, circling and pulsing until I'm sure my poor heart may explode. The soft bristle of his top lip tickles me delicately and I lift my head closer, wanting more of whatever it is that's happening to us. This is more than goosebumps; this kiss is dreamlike and momentous and seeps through my entire being and floods my soul. This is how I always imagined a kiss would be.

It was Shakespeare who said that the path to true love never did run smooth, and he wasn't kidding—the awkward angle of our kiss is starting to put a strain on my windpipe and making it rather difficult to breathe. It's not long before I'm on the verge of suffocating and I have no choice but to jerk my mouth away from Toby's and break the bond of our kiss. His eyes stretch wide with shock and surprise—whether that's because we kissed or because I pulled away I couldn't say, but we simply stare at each other, both too terrified and confused to speak.

"I . . . I couldn't . . . um . . . sorry Toby . . . ," I stutter crazily, sucking in great lungfuls of precious oxygen.

"Don't be sorry," he says, springing to his feet.

He stabs the stop button on the CD player and the music dies. I wish it were me instead.

"I didn't mean that I was sorry . . . ," I jabber dismally.

"You don't have to explain, Ellie. It was a stupid, spur-of-the-moment thing. I guess I'm feeling a lot more vulnerable than I realized and needed some human contact. I was just reaching out."

Human contact? Reaching out? Is that what that was? I reckon a hug would have about done it then, mate, I think to myself, smarting from his quick dismissal of what just happened between us.

"Well if that's what it was then we'll just leave it at that, shall we?' I reply curtly, jumping from the floor and seizing my bag at the door. 'I really have to get going. You know . . . Anna . . . grounded . . . blahblah."

I make a mad dash for the door and home. Two snogs in just as many weeks! My life has become one big obstacle race. Pity I lost sight of the finishing line a long time ago.

Chapter 9
Family Ties

For the next few days, Toby and I successfully avoid each other. During lunch breaks he flees to the safety of the footy field and after school I head for the library so that we don't have to face each other and the walk home. Even though I don't feel ready to confront him just yet, my days are undeniably dull and bare without him. I've replayed the mental image of our kiss back in my mind like some zealous detective—all the while searching for clues and hints as to what really took place. I've examined the dredged-up evidence until I was sure my head would plop off, but the only conclusion I can reach is that Toby definitely regrets what happened between us. After all, the words he used to describe our kiss were "stupid" and "spur of the moment," so it doesn't take a rocket scientist to realize that it definitely wasn't a milestone event in Toby's life. Now that's dead and buried I'm left to consider how the memory of our kiss will or won't affect our friendship. Will it change things forever? My first two snogs have brought me nothing but trouble, so from now on I'm keeping my lips to myself.

Frannie has been uncharacteristically absent for the past few days. I've tried calling but her mobile is always switched off, and when I try her home number Maria simply says that she's catching up on some quiet time. Quiet time? I thought only fogies needed quiet time. Even my mum doesn't need quiet time yet. So with the lads permanently on the footy pitch and Frannie at home catching up on her QT, I'm forced to spend my lunch breaks with double-crossing, witchy-woman Pearl. I don't feel much like talking to her, but that's not really a problem because Pearl is content to gas away and doesn't expect me to say anything back. As long as there's an ear somewhere in the near vicinity Pearl is happy to wag her jaws, and I'm only sitting with her because I have nowhere else to be.

"And anyway," Pearl natters on while I play tag with the thoughts zigzagging around in my head, "so I said that he should come and spend his breaks with us. After all, what are cousins for?" I may not be interested in Pearl's prattle but I don't trust her one bit and my ears are on red alert for the words "Glen" or "cousin." And the alarm has just sounded.

"What?" I splutter.

"You haven't been listening to a word I've said, have you!" Pearl clucks, showing me her tongue.

"Of course I have," I gulp, "I just didn't quite catch that last bit."

"I said," she begins, pausing for effect, "that Glen's mates are on a cricket tour and since he's new to the school and doesn't know that many people I've invited him to spend his lunch breaks with us."

My belly does a flick-flack and my nerves crackle with static at the news. "And . . . uh . . . what did he say?" I squeak.

"He said he'd love to!" Pause. "And then he asked if you'd be there." Pearl leers at me mischievously. A poisonous feeling of dread suddenly grabs me in a vice-like grip. Which way to the library?

"Hello ladies," a deep voice rumbles from above, squeezing a yelp from my gullet. Too late, it's Cyclops! Could these paving stones I am currently sitting on please open up and swallow me whole? But my prayer to the god of pavements goes unheard and gobby Glen drops down between us.

"Did I surprise you, Ella? It is Ella, isn't it?" he asks innocently, firing up a big toothy smirk. I've always hated dimples.

You know full well that my name is Ella, you big smelly ponce—and we have met, remember: You stuck your tongue down my throat, I feel like saying but don't. "Of course you didn't surprise me!" I gripe indignantly.

"I was just telling Ella about this gorgeous guy I met on an Internet chat site called Chat Up," Pearl gushes, looking to me for confirmation. She was?

"Yes, she was," I smile at Cyclops lamely, although I don't have the foggiest notion what she's talking about. Gorgeous guy? Chat Up? "How do you know he's gorgeous if you've never seen him?" I ask reasonably.

"Oh, there you go! Hold on to your hats everyone because Ella Mental is on the case! Can't you just be happy for me?" Pearl blazes with sudden anger.

"I'm not . . . on the case, that is. And I am . . . happy for you, that is," I answer, feeling stupid. I feel rather uncomfortable with Cyclops around.

"I've just never heard you mention this Internet guy before and I'm interested, that's all."

"If you were listening to me earlier you would know!" Pearl retorts. Her recent love glow has been darkened by her fury at my lack of enthusiasm.

"Well, I'd also like to hear about this guy," chirps Cyclops, giving me a wink, "so start again from the beginning."

I get the impression that Glen thinks he's coming to my rescue. If only he knew that the only way he could come to my rescue was if he emigrated to Australia and took Beastly Becky with him.

Not one to miss out on the opportunity to talk about herself, Pearl conveniently forgets her huff and starts chattering away about this guy called Tatty. Everyone calls him Tatty because he's seriously into grunge and also a tattoo artist. One of the best in the county, Pearl is quick to add.

"So how old is he then?" I ask casually.

"About seventeen or eighteen or something," she answers with a shrug. "Age is just a number so I don't bother asking really. He's also into body piercing!"

Peabody Public Library
Columbia City, IN

This Tatty sounds like a right yob, but if being friends with Pearl has taught me anything, it's to consider the consequences of my words before I open my mouth. Think before you talk—that's Good Sense Guide number twenty-five. Some things are better left unsaid and really aren't worth the trouble, and this is a prime example. And what do I know about romance and relationships anyway, I reflect—gazing out across the football field and wishing myself anywhere but here.

The angels must have a plan because Toby chooses that exact same moment to glance in my direction. Our eyes catch and lock and the air particles between us hiss and crackle with a charge of energy. I feel as if the rest of the human population has been zapped into the atmosphere (and Pearl and her cheesy cousin are the first to go), leaving Toby and me alone at last. I could sit staring, savoring our connection forever, but the magic moment is quickly ruined by Cyclops, who—for some unknown reason—is still sitting beside me and suddenly tugging on my ponytail. And even though I know he's only trying to be playful, as Toby turns his back on me I feel like I could kick Glen's rear end from here to the moon.

• • •

Mum's car isn't in the driveway and Dad plays darts on Thursdays but Anna's still grounded so I'm not surprised to find her home and tucked up in front of the telly with Dog. "You fancy a cuppa?" I ask as I bypass the living room. We don't really do the greeting thing.

"Yeah, go on," she answers from her dent in the couch.

I make us each a mug and join her in front of the telly where Buffy the Vampire Slayer is blow-dried and lip-glossed and busy giving some creature of the night what for with a swift kick of her designer heel. Dog is having a dream about some hunk of the canine world, luxuriously flexing her doggy toes and howling softly to herself. It must be a really good dream. "When are you out on parole?" I ask my sibling.

"Next weekend, thank goodness," Anna sighs in answer to my question. "You wouldn't believe how much I miss Spencer."

Try me, I think to myself morbidly, roasting my lip on the hot tea. I haven't told anybody that I kissed my best friend and for the moment that skeleton has been crammed right into the back of the cupboard. What choice do I have? I'm surrounded by self-centred bigheads. Come to think of it: I'm ticked off with Toby too. So what if he was feeling vulnerable? Why did he have to go and snog me of all people anyway? Doesn't the name Ella Mental mean anything to anybody any more? I've got to try get over this.

"So how was the weekend with Spencer?" I ask nonchalantly, although inside I'm really busting a gut to know how far she actually went with him.

"Oh, the whole parental unit harassment thing was like soooo embarrassing." She rolls her eyes and pouts like she's a famous film star instead of a hormone-struck, small-town teenager.

"Apart from that!" I order impatiently.

"Well, let's just say that it was very cozy and very romantic!" she smirks.

Ha, still a virgin! She'd never be able to resist lording that one over me, I chortle inwardly. The door swings open and Mum arrives home. Her arms are weighed down with grocery bags so I get up to help her carry them in but don't say anything.

"Hello, Ella!" she trumpets, making it sound more like an order. She can't even greet me without bossing me about.

"Hi," I mutter as I pass Anna carrying the few

remaining bags into the kitchen. Anna doesn't seem bothered by her punishment or about very much, in fact—and I envy her new carefree attitude. We both abandon the grocery bags on the counter and head straight back to Dog and the couch, where we attempt to watch our favorite soapie over the deafening ruckus coming from the kitchen. Mum is putting the shopping away and preparing dinner with a serious dose of attitude—intent on showing her daughters as well as the locals in far-flung Mongolia that she's miffed that we haven't offered to help her unpack.

Dad turns into the driveway twenty minutes later and strides in through the front door shortly thereafter. He spies Anna and me and grunts as if this is something unusual—like we're usually out cruising the streets of Dunton, trashing post boxes and spraying graffiti on buildings or something. Anna's flair for the dramatic is obviously inherited.

"Mmm," we both mumble from the couch but barely look up.

"Where's your mother?" he asks grimly, adding his car keys to the pile of post on the hall table and scratching through the bills with a sour look on his face.

"Making our tea," says Anna, still staring at the telly where a brunette with Tupperware breasticles is telling her boss exactly what he can do with his job.

"Miranda!" he hollers in the general direction of the kitchen.

Mum appears seconds later, wiping her hands on a checkered dishcloth and half-smiling expectantly. She leans forward to land him a kiss and he hands her a white sheet of A4 paper from a plastic folder. "I got the receptionist to type it up," he says to her and then turns to us. "We're having a family meeting, girls," he calmly announces and ushers Mum into the living room. "These," he begins, doling out two more sheets of paper, "are for each of you."

We both hesitate and then reach for the sheets gingerly—like they're explosive letter bombs that might go off in our faces. And we're not far wrong, because one side of the paper is printed with a list of numbered points, and centered at the top are the horrifying words: "REVISED HOUSE RULES."

Anna and I stare at the list and then slowly and painfully turn to face one another. This can't be happening; not now! We've only just been allowed to attend school socials! If Dad has noticed our pasty, sickened expressions he doesn't let on (or he just doesn't care), and with a quick, self-important rumble in his throat, he begins the speech we just know he's been sitting on for days.

"Your mum and I really thought that we could trust you girls," he says, and then pauses for effect, "but it seems we were sorely mistaken. So things are about to change around here, I'm very sorry to say."

Oh yeah right you are, I grimace and air-mail a disgusted look in Anna's direction. Every bit of this is her fault!

"From now on you will both take careful notice of this revised list of house rules, which I will also tape to the fridge door, so that it's in sight as a reminder. Now, starting from the top . . ."

REVISED HOUSE RULES

Weekdays: you will return home immediately after school & complete all homework. Only then may you go out again. You will be home by 5:30 p.m.

Weekends: you will be home by no later than 9:30 p.m.

No watching television before 5 p.m. Non-negotiable!

Mum has joined the school parents' committee and volunteered her services as a parent chaperone at the school socials. You are allowed to attend any school social events she is chaperoning.

You are allowed to sleep out once a month, but only if and when we have discussed it with your friend's parents beforehand.

We require three days' prior notice of your plans to sleep out.

When sleeping at a friend's house you are banned from going out anywhere. Your friends' parents will be notified of this fact beforehand too.

When you leave the house ensure your mobile is charged, switched on, and within reach at all times. A dead battery will result in punishment.

You will both be expected to help out around the house more. A revised list of chores to follow.

Chapter 10
Mad Cow Disease

I have the entire weekend ahead of me and not a single thing to do. Anna has already made a break for it and is making the most of her new-found freedom with Marcia, and Toby . . . well, enough said. I feel like I haven't breathed for weeks and think I may burst a blood vessel if I don't have some contact with him soon. I must have my best friend back and disregard the fact that for a very short while we were something more. And at least it will get me out of this combat zone, if nothing else.

Just the thought of seeing Toby causes my insides to wobble about like half-set jelly. I've never been this nervous for anything in my life. It's almost eleven o'clock and I wonder if I'll even find him at home. The driveway is empty, which means that both his parents are out—that's presuming that they're both still living there, of course. Who knows what's happened since we last spoke. So mustering up all my courage and thinking about everything under the sun except sprinting all the way back home again, I march straight up to the front door and ring the doorbell. Silence. I will not chicken out. Just as I'm about to ring the bell a second time the door suddenly swings open and I find myself staring directly at Daftcow Melanie. She's usually too high and mighty to slum it and play doorman, so I can only presume that Toby's not home after all.

"Well hi, Ella Mental," Melanie croons. "I saw you coming down the road and guessed that you were on your way to pay us a visit. Aren't we the lucky ones?"

"Uh, yah," I answer, indifferent to what she thinks and wishing she'd stop grinning at me like that. Never trust anyone who is too nice, they're either insincere fakes or they want something from you—that's Good Sense Guide number five, and I learnt it from Daftcow Melanie a long time ago. "Toby's out, is he?" I ask.

"Oh no, Toby's very much at home!" she says, fluttering her mascara-congealed eyelashes at me. "He's got a visitor—Becky. I'm not sure he wants to be disturbed."

A lethal cocktail of shock, pain, anger, and fear dissolves my insides instantly, leaving me giddy with nausea. Beastly Becky here? But . . . since when? My head overflows with the startling mental image of Becky and Toby lying in front of his CD player, their heads together, resting on the blue continental pillow that matches the bedspread and curtains . . . her blonde hair mixing with his. She's probably barefoot and tapping her pretty painted toes to the music. My scalp and fingertips begin to tingle and the hole in my belly starts fizzing and popping as if I've swallowed a whole packet of tom-thumb firecrackers.

"Is there anything else?" Melanie asks.

"Er . . . no," I say, twisting away quickly before she can see the hot tears erupting from my eyes and sliding down my cheeks like molten lava. My vision is wet and blurry and I'm forced to negotiate my way out of the Sinclair front garden using only my memory and intuition. I don't hear the door close behind me and I imagine that Melanie is still standing there and staring at my sad, staggering figure.

I find my way to the park and flop down beneath a gigantic oak tree, resting my back against its rough corrugated bark. My mouth is dry but my hands are soggy—as if my saliva has been sucked out through the pores in my palms (it's not uncommon for me to think peculiar thoughts when I'm going to pieces). A weightless wind is swirling and gossiping with the leaves overhead and gently drying my tears, and after a while I slowly start to feel calmer. And as my panic subsides I'm able to start sorting through the various strands of emotion that have exploded all over the place.

"I don't get upset when Pearl or Frannie visit Toby, and they're also girls," I say to myself reasonably.

"Yes, but Pearl and Frannie aren't interested in being anything more than Toby's friend, are they?" the little green-eyed monster sitting on my left shoulder replies. Mmm, Miss Green Eyes has a point.

"Well, I was very happy and content when I was just Toby's friend. That's all that really matters to me," I respond reasonably.

"And that's exactly why," Green Eyes seethes through clenched teeth, "we aren't ready for Toby to have a girlfriend!"

Game, set, and match to the green-eyed monster on my left. And that's exactly it! If Toby gets a girlfriend it will change absolutely everything and I'll lose the one and only true friend I have in this entire wretched world. But all my rationalizing still doesn't fully explain the mysterious and dreadful pain that's threatening to crush my chest. I sit quietly and try to listen instead of think, and that's when I understand. Buried somewhere deep inside me was the belief that one day our friendship would grow into something more. I've hero-worshipped Toby my entire life, ever since we were kids baking mud pies and playing kiss chase, and subconsciously I've always taken it for granted that one day we would fall in love and remain together for ever and ever. In my perfect world I could never lose Toby to somebody else if he didn't just love me as a friend, but was in love with me too. The sad reality of the situation is a bit like discovering that Father Christmas is really a fat, balding, out-of-work used-car salesman, and something I don't know that I'll ever recover from.

A group of kids about my age arrive at the park and start messing about and smoking cigarettes. I recognize them from school and even though I don't have much to do with them I really don't want them to see me sitting alone sobbing underneath a dumb tree. And considering that I genuinely have been worried about Frannie, I decide that concentrating on someone else's troubles for a while might help take my mind off my own. Everything new seems scary to begin with and bad news is like most things in life—you need time to adjust to it. That's Good Sense Guide number eight and something I've learnt from experience. So dusting off my bottom as well as my battered ego, I set off in the direction of the Mendes' household.

Frannie's mum answers my knock and solemnly ushers me indoors. The house is cold and silent and there's a heavy feeling of apprehension in the air, like someone's terminally ill or something.

"Is everything all right?" I ask.

"You're just the person I wanted to see, Ella dear," she smiles limply, ignoring my question. "Come take a seat. Would you like something to drink?"

Actually I would, but right now dehydration takes a back seat to my fear at discovering that I'm just the person she wants to see, so I wiggle my head. This can't be good; people don't usually want to see me. I'm suddenly overwhelmed by the urge to yell: "It wasn't me!" and do a runner, but I expect it'll be more believable if I at least wait and hear what she has to say first.

"Ella, have you noticed anything different about Francisca lately?"

Maria's Portuguese accent seems especially thick today and it takes a few moments for her question to penetrate my brain. The solemn look on her face tells me that this is extremely serious and I really want to answer correctly, so I stare at the ceiling (I concentrate much better when I stare at the ceiling), and think things through carefully. Of course I've noticed a change in Frannie. She's temperamental and emotionally all over the place: up one moment and in the doldrums the next. I realize that teenagers are by definition supposed to be moody, but lately Frannie seems to have more issues than *CosmoGIRL!* And it's definitely not like her to miss school. Perhaps she's in some sort of trouble, although I have no idea what it could be. I don't want to say anything that could make things any worse for her or land her in trouble either.

"Yes, sort of . . . I guess so," I answer cagily, eager to straddle the fence as long as possible. Maria is studying me carefully over the rim of her spectacles, which is making me feel very uncomfortable indeed. "Has she said anything to you?" I ask, strategically shifting the attention away from myself and on to the poor, distressed mother sitting before me.

"No, she won't talk to me," Maria sighs. "Francisca just sits in her room. She doesn't want to eat, to go out, or do anything. I have tried everything I can think of but she says she just wants to be left alone. Perhaps that's normal for someone of your age. Do you also just want to be left alone?"

Actually I'm getting a bit fed up with being deserted all the time, but it's not really the same thing and I almost feel as sorry for Frannie's mum as I do for myself. "When did you first start noticing the change in Frannie?" I ask her.

Maria looks baffled for a moment or two and fiddles nervously with the hem of her skirt. "I'm not sure, really. It didn't happen overnight. I've been very busy for the past few months helping my brother settle down in England. It's been so difficult for him to say goodbye to Portugal, you know, but now he's living around the corner and everything is finally back to normal. Perhaps Francisca feels neglected. I've tried to explain things to her but she says that she doesn't care. So I just don't know."

I finally understand Maria's pain; she so badly wants to make everything perfect for Frannie, but she can't until she knows what—if anything—is bothering her only child. I think we must be the two saddest people in the entire world. "I tell you what," I say uncertainly. "I'll see if Frannie wants to speak to me. I don't know that she will, but I'll do what I can."

Maria leans over and gently taps the top of my hand. "You're a good girl," she smiles softly. She's got a real motherliness about her and for a brief moment I want to curl up against her and let our two rivers of problems flow into one. I know she would give me good advice, but right now I think she's got enough to cope with and so I stand up and head for Frannie's room instead. The door is firmly shut and I knock softly.

"Maaam, please leave me to sleep," Frannie gripes through the wall.

"It's me, Ella!" I try to sound happy and hopeful—embracing the door like I'm hugging for Greenpeace.

After a few moments of silence Frannie drones: "Oh. Okay. You'd better come in."

Her room is dark and stale and I can just make out her gloomy shape beneath the quilted mound on her bed. "Frannie, are you feeling sick?" I ask directly. The scene is too startling for polite chitchat.

"No, I'm just tired," she says, heaving another enormous sigh.

"It's very dark in here," I say slowly. "Shall I turn a lamp on?"

Frannie remains quiet for a while, pondering the answer to my question like she's used up all her lifelines. "Yeah, okay—if you must."

I feel my way towards her desk lamp and run my hand from the base to the cord, searching for the square box that is the on/off switch. I press it and a section of the room illuminates with a yellow glow and nets the lump on the bed in its warm fringes. At last I can see my unhappy friend a little better. Her skin is sallow, her hair could do with a wash, and the crescent-shaped smudges around her eyes have darkened. I move towards her and perch on the edge of the bed, gently draping my arm across her shoulders.

"Is there anything you want to talk about?" I ask, calmly stroking soothing circles on her back with my fingers. But Frannie remains quiet and distant and seems strangely uncomfortable with my touch, so I stop the stroking but remain where

I am, hoping my closeness will break through the barrier of isolation she's built around herself. "I probably don't have any of the answers, but sometimes just talking can make things seem better," I continue. "It's kinda like bursting a boil."

Frannie's eyeballs dart this way and that as I play catch with her gaze. "Please Frannie, why are you so down?" I plead, hoping she'll see that her depression and moodiness affects those who love her, too. Maybe she's just having a hormone overload.

"I'm not down," she eventually sniffs. "Just because I don't walk around grinning twenty-four-seven like some village idiot doesn't mean I'm down. Maybe I just need some time to think about things and sort my head out. But I don't want to talk about anything. And this goes for you and my mum, because I know you've been talking. Thanks for your concern, but just give me a bit of space, huh?"

How much space, I wonder? Enough to see her through the weekend; enough to park a bus in; or does she really mean "don't call me, I'll call you"? "That's fine, Fran. But I'm always here if you ever need to talk," I reply, getting up from her bed and feeling just a little bit silly. "I'll see you at school," I whisper as I close the door behind me.

I'm officially the loneliest person alive. My stomach feels like it's been vacuum-packed and I'm suddenly in desperate need of some emotionally fulfilling junk food. Of course I realize that choosing Ronald MacDonald for my therapist and counsellor is probably not the wisest decision I could make, but how else do I take my mind off the whirlpool of emotions swirling sickly in my belly?

Chapter 11
Grapevine of Wrath

John Bennie is the first person I see at school on Monday and I notice that he still has some faint purple around his left eye where Alf stamped his signature on to his face with his fist. It makes him look even more thuggish and terrifying than usual. His neck is as thick as a boa constrictor snaking out of his broad, chunky shoulders and the hair on his head is pale and bristly and inter-sected by a thin, naked scar that runs from his crown to his right ear. I stay away from John Bennie and he treats me as if I simply don't exist, which of course I'm rather grateful for. He's look-ing particularly arrogant and challenging today, so I make an extra-special point of staying out of his way.

Unfortunately John Bennie's not the only one who thinks I'm invisible. My close-encounter-of-the-third-kind with Frannie and the discovery that Toby and Becky are officially a couple has left me feeling abandoned and worthless. I've lost my two best friends, how could I feel anything else? It's getting so bad that even Cyclops is starting to look appealing. But with a geography assignment that's due in a week's time I decide to escape to the library in the name of research. Being lonely is less noticeable in libraries, and there's zero chance of me bumping into BB and Toby there. Becky's probably still memorizing the alphabet anyway.

I really enjoy spending time in our school library, even when I do have friends. There's something very peaceful and unthreatening about a place where knowledge is power and books are the keys that open the doors to a million different places, times, and people far more interesting than my own miserable existence. And I somehow feel safer surrounded by bookworm types. They seem to be a calmer, kinder and more tolerant lot, and owning a library card is almost like belonging to their secret society. As long as you know your Dewey Decimal and the rules of the Reference Section and you don't refer to anyone who is visually challenged as "four-eyes," then you're a keeper (even if you do have spots, flat feet, or thighs that wobble like a possessed pudding).

Today the usual peace and quiet of the library seems strangely disturbed. The solid, upstanding bookcases—usually so stern and silent—appear alive with whispers and mutterings, like a hibernating monster that's slowly stirring to life. Every nook and cranny is buzzing with clusters of book lovers—usually so voiceless and obedient—nattering and murmuring in hushed tones. At first I try to ignore the rumblings, determinedly scanning the PYs for something interesting on Pygmies (for my geography assignment—I have no personal interest in them, although I'm sure they're really nice people). But after a while the brief snatches of sentences stolen here and there are just too much to disregard and I feel compelled to investigate. Something major must have happened for this lot to get excited.

I decide to head straight for the root of the grapevine: the gossiping librarians. Directly alongside the book check-in and -out counter is a tall magazine rack, which provides me with the perfect opportunity to eavesdrop on the librarians undetected. I sink to my haunches and pretend to scan the titles on the bottom shelf before grabbing any old magazine, which I start flicking through mindlessly—straining my ears for scraps of information. As only my luck would have it, I just happen to have picked up a copy of a self-help magazine for teenage boys called *Boys To Men*, and this particular issue has the words "Puberty and Your Erections" emblazoned in dazzling colors across its cover. Mortified, I speedily swap it for the latest issue of *PC Power* and scan the surrounding area to determine whether anybody has noticed my fumbling. But I needn't have worried; everyone is too busy with their chitchat.

"No, I don't know his surname! All I know is that his first name is Tom," the librarian with the red hair and freckles hisses at her librarian friend.

"And do they know who did it?" her friend whispers back. I can't see her face but if the tone of her voice is anything to go by I imagine her eyes are as big as satellite dishes.

"No, he won't say," Redhead answers with authority, "but word is that it was John Bennie and his mates. It seems they've been picking on this Tom for a while."

Like salt sprinkled on a snail the mention of Tom's name makes my heart shrivel and dry up in my chest. How many other Toms could John Bennie possibly be bullying, I wonder with panic, but still hoping with every fiber in my body that it's not my dear, sweet Tom-Tom they're talking about. But what happened? What did John Bennie and his brutal and senseless cronies do? I hold my breath—just in case I should miss anything by inhaling.

A brand new voice arrives on the scene to ask if she can pay her fine next week but still take books out this week blab blabbety blab. Go away stupid girl, I want to scream! I'm gripping the copy of *PC Power* so tightly my knuckles are blanched as white as my face. Just take the flaming books and scram! There's a small chance I may need a few classes in anger management when this is all over. After what seems like an age the two gossiping librarians eventually return to their story.

"The poor lad," Redhead continues, obviously referring to Tom, "when McLachlan found him it seems he'd wet himself." I know Mr. McLachlan; he's our school caretaker.

"You . . . are . . . kidding!" Redhead's friend chugs.

"No really! They tied him up with skipping ropes nicked from the gym and once they were done they just left him. I don't know what would have happened if McLachlan hadn't gone down to the basement boiler room when he did. A person could die down there!" Redhead exclaims dramatically.

I cannot take another single second of this. "DIE?!" I jump up from behind the counter and shriek at the top of my voice. The copy of *PC Power* somersaults high into the air but nobody seems to notice. My sudden and very vocal appearing act has terrified both Redhead and her friend witless. They scream with fear and simultaneously raise their arms in the air, as if they're in a stick-up. Some of us definitely need to spend less time browsing the Thrillers section.

"You have to tell me everything you know about Tom-Tom," I say breathlessly.

"Who is Tom-Tom?" Redhead and her friend squeak.

Time has slowed down to mush. "Tom-Tom is Tom—the guy you were just talking about. He's a friend of mine. What happened?" I ask again.

"Ooooh . . . ," they croon and slowly lower their raised arms.

"Well," begins Redhead, once again confident and eager to be heard, "what I was told is that John Bennie and his crew tied this Tom to a chair and then did all sorts of disgusting things to him. They force-fed him a mixture of dog doo, cigarettes, and baked beans; they peed on his shoes; and they smeared No-Hair all over his head. And then they disappeared, leaving him there for McLachlan to find."

Mum uses No-Hair instead of a razor to remove the hair on her legs and so I know how bad it smells and how it makes her itch like crazy. As I think about Tom-Tom and the torture he endured a great feeling of sadness seeps through my entire being and evaporates my insides, leaving me filled with an emptiness that hurts. "When did this happen?" I whisper.

"Yesterday afternoon," Redhead answers matter-of-factly, gawking at me as if she's expecting stegosaurus eggs to hatch out of my eye sockets.

I stumble towards the library exit, desperate to find Tom-Tom and Toby. I need to make sure that Tom-Tom is okay, and Toby will know how to fix everything. The bright light of the outside feels like a thousand toothpicks piercing my eyeballs, making them water like crazy. Or else I'm crying. Or perhaps it's a bit of both. We should have known that John Bennie wouldn't take a bruising without evening the score. This is his payback.

As I head towards the quad I pass clumps of chattering kids, and I know without a doubt what it is they're talking about. Like some evil demon the story has possessed the pupils at Dunton, and it's growing stronger and more powerful with every tongue and ear it touches. I track it snaking a path across the soccer pitch, the players stopping mid-air and their jaws dropping to the ground, the ball—for once—forgotten. In the school canteen it weaves its way across the sturdy rectangular eating tables and knocks the chewing children like dominoes. Each one looks more shocked than the last, although every so often I spy a wicked sneer in place of a gasp of pity. Some kids are taking pleasure in Tom-Tom's tragedy, and for the first time in my life I understand that the world is made up of good and bad people. But the bad ones live, breathe, eat and look just like the good ones so that you wouldn't know if you were sitting beside one or not. This realization chips away a small piece of my childhood innocence and mashes it to powder.

I eventually find Pearl sitting with Cyclops and Frannie, who looks astonishingly scrubbed up and back to her normal self again, although it appears as if she may cry, so I guess she's already heard the dreadful news. They probably all knew before I did. An anxious Toby and a snarling Alfie arrive just a few moments later and there's no doubt that they know too.

"What are we going to do?" I wail desperately, trying to control my emotions and not act like a big baby.

"We're going to thump 'em!" roars Alfie, baring his teeth in hate.

"We've got to see if Tom-Tom is okay before we do anything," Toby orders firmly. "Come on— let's go!"

"But where?" I cry. I'm not handling this as well as I could.

"Well he's not at school so he must be at home!" blares Alfie, still running on rage.

"But we'll get caught bunking!" gulps Frannie.

"Who cares!" insists Toby. "Tom-Tom needs us right now and we have to see for ourselves that he's okay!"

I just knew Toby would be wonderful and brave. Everyone nods in agreement and in a matter of minutes we've escaped the school grounds and are heading towards the outskirts of the estate where Tom-Tom lives with his mum and younger brother. There's nothing like a crisis to bring people together, and the five of us sweep into Tom-Tom's road, striding shoulder to shoulder like a band of courageous vigilantes. We pull up at his house and catch Tom-Tom's mum, dressed in her pale green and blue Marks & Spencer's uniform and leaving for work. She looks weary and downtrodden and her face has the wrung-out look of someone who's spent the night crying instead of sleeping.

"Tom is inside. He's doing okay, but I don't know that he's up to seeing you all just now," she says, subconsciously barring our way like a lioness protecting her wounded cub. She still has a faint trace of a Caribbean accent that years of living in England haven't yet managed to wipe away. She doesn't seem surprised to see us, but then I wonder if anything will surprise her ever again. "We want him to know that we're here for him," Toby replies, sounding somber but sincere.

This makes Tom-Tom's mum smile sadly. "I know you are guys. But there's more to it than that, and I think that Tom just needs to be left alone for a while. Please trust me on this one."

No one seems to know what to say next, but before any one of us can find a voice for the desperate questions slamming around in our skulls, the door suddenly and unexpectedly unlocks from the inside and swings wide open to reveal Tom-Tom, silhouetted against the backlight like some transported angel. "It's okay, Mum. I'll be okay." His deep voice hums reassuringly from the shadows.

Mrs Toisin gazes at the vague outline in the doorway for a moment, blows her son a kiss and then strides briskly down the path without saying another word.

"I think this is affecting her more than it is me," the voice from the gloom speaks again, standing aside to let us pass.

Only once inside are we finally able to see Tom-Tom clearly. His usual head of thick, curly black hair has been shaved down to dark fuzz. It changes his face completely, or seems to anyway.

"Ah, my new hairdo . . ." Tom-Tom smiles feebly and tentatively touches his shorn head. We've obviously all been staring without meaning to or realizing it. "A change is as good as a holiday, huh?" he adds, trying to make light of it. His courage makes me queasy and I want to hug him tightly enough to make new curly hair sprout from his scalp. Be angry, be sad, scream blue, pink, and green murder, but please don't be so silent and strong.

"It looks cool, man!" Alfie grins, breaking from the mourning circle and heading for one of the floral couches nearby.

"I'll put the kettle on," offers Pearl, hurrying into the kitchen before anyone can refuse. Not that any of us would. When you're English every crisis requires tea. We all trail Alfie into the living area where the television is on and showing a muted gardening program. A man in a plaid shirt is planting saplings in rich dark soil, and the image is mesmerizing and strangely reassuring. But it doesn't plug my fear. I make a point of remaining in Toby's line of sight—we need each other now more than ever—but he seems to be making a point of blurring me out. Soon Pearl emerges from the kitchen carrying a tray loaded with mismatched steaming mugs and an enormous yellow sugar bowl, but nobody moves to switch the telly off.

"I want you guys to know one thing," Tom-Tom rallies against the quiet. "I didn't pee myself because I was scared. I pee'd myself because I needed to pee . . . but couldn't get my hands free."

Every single one of us remains stock-still,

staring at the floor, walls, or ceiling—anywhere but at Tom-Tom, as if we are personally to blame for his ordeal.

"I just wanted you all to know that," Tom-Tom repeats softly. Silence.

"When you gotta go you gotta go, huh buddy?" Toby finally chirps, his handsome face splitting with a gigantic grin. Perhaps a little too gigantic, but it dissolves some of the tension and puts us all at ease, and for a very brief moment we're back to being six carefree kids hanging out with nothing more on our minds than making it home in time for supper. But the mood doesn't last long. That would be impossible. Nice. But impossible.

"Everyone says it was John Bennie and his idiots who did this to you. Is that true?" Alfie demands, a look of surly determination gripping his face.

Tom-Tom remains quiet for a moment, holding Alfie's gaze with his own and considering how best to respond. "I don't want this thing to carry on," he answers simply.

"That's not what I asked," Alfie yaps, not budging an inch.

"You know it was. Who else could it be?" Tom-Tom eventually answers. "But this isn't your fight, Alf. This isn't anybody's fight—not even mine. I know enough to know that people only bully because they're unhappy within themselves. This really has nothing to do with me, or the fact that my skin is darker than his. John Bennie is a miserable sod. He's miserable with himself and his lot in life, and he's miserable because he's failing school. He's attacking me to take his mind off the fact that he's a weak, spineless loser. That's why people bully. Strong, happy people don't bully."

We sit there astounded by the mature monologue Tom-Tom's just delivered, although Alfie doesn't seem able to decide whether he's impressed or annoyed by Tom-Tom's mellow dismissal of John Bennie's psychosis.

"That's a very philosophical way of looking at things," I blurt out. Tom-Tom's right. When I'm unhappy within myself I'm far less tolerant and much more aggressive towards others. How you treat other people is a direct reflection of how you feel about yourself! That's so obvious, why didn't I see it before? I'll definitely add that to the Good Sense Guide.

"Well, I suppose I should come clean and admit that I didn't exactly feel this way yesterday," Tom-Tom growls, suddenly looking murderous. "Yesterday I wanted to taste John Bennie's blood and slaughter him for the humiliation he caused me. But my mum and I stayed up talking until four this morning, and she helped me to understand a lot of things. Some of what I just told you, but a few other things too. Like, have you guys ever wondered why I don't have a dad?"

We glance at each other blankly and roll our shoulders. "I thought your dad disappeared when you were a kid," Pearl guesses.

"And I suppose I just didn't say anything to make you believe otherwise," Tom-Tom continues. "But the truth is that my dad died six months after my first birthday. Well, he didn't just die. He was murdered . . . stabbed five times in the back by two drunken guys who couldn't deal with the fact that he was black and spoke with an accent and was sitting having a beer in the same pub as them. They didn't think that was right, and so they attacked him and left my mum with one baby and another on the way."

The revelation numbs us into silence. Suddenly Tom-Tom seems larger than life. "I'm so sorry man," Toby eventually mutters. "But it's good to know that you don't hold any grudges because of it."

"No way!" Tom-Tom answers speedily. "How many times have you heard about a black guy wasting another black guy because he's in a different crew or something? Plenty! Black, white, and anything in between . . . we're all as bad and as good as each other. My mum taught me that. Only ignorance and stupidity breeds hate, nothing else. And hate will drain you, man. It will leave you empty. God gave us free will; free will to think and choose for ourselves—that's what separates us from wild animals. And I choose to exercise my free will and live by my rules—not by John Bennie's. I don't need to behave like a savage just because he does."

Chapter 12
Keeping Up Appearances

Lately the weekends only serve to remind me of one thing: that I have a seriously irritating family. Living in this house is an extreme sport. And it seems to be getting worse. The units are swanning about looking mightily chuffed with themselves and the fact that they've managed to transform our teenage years into the most claustrophobic and dreary experience imaginable. And Anna seems to be as loopy as the units, which may mean that insanity is hereditary (in which case, please just shoot me). She's not interested in anything any more, and that includes me, school, sleeping, me, food, me, or anything that doesn't spell S-P-E-N-C-E-R. My two best friends and my twin sister all think I'm invisible. So I try to keep to myself and my bedroom, and the parental units think I'm miserable and ungrateful and regularly give each other sympathetic knowing looks until I want to holler and rip my ears off in frustration.

But all the madness of the past few days has

given me a new perspective on life and inspired me to take my own advice: When the going gets tough you can either roll over and play dead or you can rise to the challenge and take a few knocks, but emerge stronger and wiser for it. So it may be the plot for a thousand Hollywood blockbusters, but it's also Elemental Good Sense Guide logic.

I'm missing Toby so much that if I sit around moping I'll definitely trip my switches. He's the only person I feel completely relaxed around and I miss that carefree ease we have with each other. Being me has always been good enough for Toby. It's not good enough for most other people, but Toby always seemed to like me just fine. It's been days and weeks since we've spoken properly—just the two of us, like we used to—and it's left a gaping hole in my life. So my strategy is to do absolutely everything possible to win Toby over. I know that he loves me more than he loves dingbat Becky; he just needs a little reminder. I'm going to prove to him that I'm prettier, nicer, and far more intelligent that she could ever hope to be, although I don't think I'll have to do much to prove I'm more intelligent. That's not vanity (even Dog has that base covered). And I'm quite sure I'm nicer than her too, though I have to admit that Becky's sort of easy on the eye. If you're into trim girls with ballerina legs, long sandy hair, and high cheekbones, that is. But surely brains and personality count for something more? Still, from now on I'm going to start eating healthily and exercise this bod into shape. This is just mind over matter, and if she can do it then so can I.

All the mags say that you should know how much you weigh, so that'll be the first step in my makeover. Anna hoards the scales in her bedroom, which means that I'll probably need to send out a search party to find it first. It's impossible to scrounge things from my sister any more because these days her bedroom looks like the aftermath of a end-of-season fashion sale. It used to be so easy—I could be in and out of her cupboard in a matter of seconds without her even noticing—but nowadays I'm lucky if I can find the floor. If love is a sickness, then her case is terminal.

It takes me almost five minutes to locate the scales lurking beneath a smoldering pile of Anna's dirty laundry that's shoved in a dark corner of her room and starting to smell like Gorgonzola. The curved window of the scales' dial is an evil, leering mouth and I pull a tongue at it spitefully. Narrowing my eyes at it, I think: *I* could crush you with one thump of my thunderous thigh, you insignificant man-made device of torture. I suck in my tummy and prepare to mount the scales just as the phone rings.

I scramble to answer it. It's not Toby. It's Pearl, calling to ask if I'd like to come around to hers for a bit. Right now I'll accept an invitation to a bonfire in hell if it means escaping this house, but before I put down the phone to Pearl I make her cross-your-heart promise that Glen a.k.a. Cyclops won't be there.

I head off to Pearl's house, which is situated in an over-developed part of the council estate. It's cramped and a bit run down, but they do their best to keep it cared for. For the most part the people who live there are really friendly and kind, although a few of the young blokes can appear rather loud and threatening. It's the ones that cruise the neighborhood in souped-up cars powered by brutal, thumping music that you want to be especially wary of. They rattle about with their chunky gold jewellery doing complicated hand-shakes and spouting the latest ghetto-speak, which they think makes them cool. And if they were bigger and a bit badder it just might, but most of them are skinny with pale, spotty skins and moth-eaten haircuts. They look more street-urchin-stupid than ghetto-fabulous, although this is an opinion I tend to keep to myself. Funny-looking dogs bite too.

The front door is opened by Pearl's grubby eight-year-old brother Dan whose mouth, I notice, is ringed with a lumpy brown crust. Please let that be peanut butter, I pray. Dan wordlessly gives my shins a good hard kick before hightailing it upstairs, leaving a trail of fiendish laughter in his wake. "Brat!" I mutter, and yank the door closed behind me. The brown gunk that's on his face is also on the door handle and now on my hand. "Pearl . . . ?" I call, wiping my mucky fingers on my jeans and listening for the yelled response that will lead me to her.

"Bedroom!" she hollers from upstairs. Teenagers generally don't need full sentences to communicate; a few well-timed keywords will go a long way.

Pearl shares a bedroom with her sister Beth—or is supposed to anyway, although she refuses to acknowledge her sister's claim to the space and always calls it "her bedroom." She's even drawn a line in chalk down the center of the room, dividing it into her "half" and Beth's "half," but percentage-wise it's not close to a fifty-fifty split and Pearl just happens to have included the wardrobe, computer, stereo, and door in her section. So every time poor Beth wants to get to her "half" she has to check that Pearl is not within flinging distance (Pearl likes to throw things) and race to her barren little corner.

I find Pearl sitting cross-legged on a chair in front of "her" computer. She's wearing her favorite Manchester United cap and typing manically on the keyboard. "A sec . . ." she murmurs, glimpsing me out of the corner of her eye. I can just make out the Chat Up website logo nestling in the top corner of the computer screen, so no prizes for guessing that Pearl and Tatty are spreading their own brand of crazy in one of the site's chatrooms. I wait patiently while she bangs out a few more sentences and then finally swivels in her chair to face me. "You look freaking awful!" she exclaims, screwing her nose up at me like I smell bad too.

"Thanks Pearl," I mutter, "and to think I came all this way to get abused when I could have stayed at home and saved myself the walk."

"No really!" Pearl blunders ahead mercilessly. "What's up with you? Is everything okay?"

Even if I did want to open up to Pearl the Scandalmonger (which I do not), everything is too scrambled up for me to find the beginning and the end of my misery anyway and I quickly fob her off with some vague reference to my dysfunctional home life instead. "Aw, my dad's gone and issued us with a list of nasty 'revised house rules,'" I explain, working two fingers on each hand like bunny ears to demonstrate that they're his words, not mine. "If we thought the units were strict before, you should see them now. They're in full throttle!" I could actually do with having a good vent and a bellow about Anna and her stupid antics, but Pearl can blab for England—and the last thing I want are our grubby domestics flapping about in the Dunton breeze.

"Is there anything I can do to help?" Pearl asks. She finds my eyes when she says this and I'm shocked to see that her interest is sincere.

"Turn me into a swimsuit model," I joke, "that'd be a start."

"Well, I don't know about that," Pearl smiles slyly as her mind ticks over, "but there is something we can do. Come with me!" She grabs her jacket and my sleeve and starts towing me in the direction of the stairs and the front door.

"Where are we going?" I gasp, lurching behind her like a fiddler crab.

"My aunt just bought the salon down the road," she reveals, stomping over crusty Dan who happens to be lying on the floor and pulling at a growing length of loose carpet thread. "She said I could come along and have something done anytime I liked—and I'm sure she won't mind if I bring a friend!"

"Something done? Like what?" I ask nervously. This is, after all, another one of Pearl's relatives we're talking about here.

"You could have some honey highlights," Pearl suggests excitedly. Honey highlights? That does sound tempting, which means that Dad will definitely disapprove. "Or how about a manicure and a pedicure?" Pearl continues, as if reading my reluctance. "Or a facial or an eyelash tint or a leg wax?"

"Slow down, you're getting delirious," I grin, suddenly equally excited at the prospect of a beautifying facial. Or perhaps a manicure and a pedicure! Watch this space, Beastly Becky!

Pearl's aunt's salon is called Sparkle Beauty Studio and the door tinkles as we enter, announcing our arrival. A thin woman with teased bouffant hair wearing passion-pink lipstick and matching open-toe, strapless heels clip-clops over to us. "Pearly!" she brays in a gravely voice that sounds like two packs a day. She gives Pearl an air-kiss and then turns to greet me with a wide grin and two of the biggest dimples I've seen . . . since . . . Cyclops. Oh hello.

"This is Simone," Pearl declares, but pronounces it See-mown, like it's foreign and posh or something.

"And you're Pearl's aunt?" I stammer, hoping against hope.

"And Glen's mum!" Pearl fills in the blanks.

"Well isn't that just great!" I burble and shake her hand, but my mouth is stiff and dry and what was meant to be a smile probably just looks like I'm suffering from Delhi-belly.

"What can I do for you ladies?" See-mown wheezes, patting the packet of Mayfair's peeking out of her breasticle pocket.

"How about Ella has her nails done and I have a facial," Pearl proposes, "and then we swap?"

"No problemo," See-mown rasps while I nod dismally. I might as well marry into this family and be done with it; it seems as though I'm never going to escape them.

147

See-mown barks an order into the air and a girl with non-existent eyebrows and a white lab coat arrives to steer me in the direction of a lilac patent-leather chair and matching footstool. I slump into the chair and Miss Tweezer-Happy starts undoing the laces of my trainers.

"Er, I can do that!" I cluck, instantly uncomfortable with the idea of her touching my feet.

"Don't worry about it, this is my job." She smiles up at me so kindly I don't have the heart to fight her for my feet. She unties my laces and gently removes my trainers and socks, and I'm suddenly grateful that today the weather is cool. I've never had anybody fiddle with my feet before and I'm sure Miss Tweezer-Happy-Sucker-For-Punishment must think they're gross.

"Now you're going to have to relax," she smiles, using all her strength to prise open my tightly curled-up toes. "Don't worry, I do this all the time," she adds reassuringly.

I let her get on with her soaking and filing and painting while I stare every which way but at her. Just about everything in the salon is a varying shade of lilac and the air smells of pot-pourri and cheap perfumed disinfectant that's definitely going to give me a headache.

"Right, now you need to sit tight and let that dry for about twenty minutes," Miss Tweezer-Happy-Sucker-For-Punishment-Feet-Lover finally instructs me. She then stands up, hands me a magazine and walks away without another word.

I flip the magazine over and glance at the cover. She's given me a copy of *Your Baby and You*. She obviously hated my feet. I open the magazine and flick this way and that, trying desperately to find something interesting to occupy the next twenty minutes, but all the articles have titles like "Getting to the Bottom of Diarrhoea" and "Beating the Breastfeeding Blues."

I look around in panic and spy a pile of magazines on the other side of the salon, but everybody around me seems super busy and I'm too embarrassed to interrupt anyone. I peek down at my new fancy feet; I've got foam wedgie-things between my toes which should stop them from touching and smudging, I reason. And it's only about eight steps to the magazines. I slide off my shiny lilac chair, making a point of walking on my heels with my toes splayed. I cover the eight or so steps without incident but the moment I lean over to grab a handful of magazines I suddenly feel a massive

149

thwack on my forehead. I stagger backwards, reeling from the painful impact and stare around me in confusion. And that's when I realize my mistake. There are no magazines at the other side of the room—it was just a reflection in the ceiling-to-floor mirror.

The loud cracking sound produced by my head hitting the glass has brought the entire salon to a halt. Everybody is staring at me with bulging frog-eyes, except for Pearl who has turned a steamy shade of hot-chilli red. Her head seems to have disappeared into her shoulders like a tortoise. Sitting beside her is See-mown a.k.a. Glen's mum a.k.a. Pearl's aunt, who—in contrast—looks like I've just made living worthwhile. "Now here's a story that's going to be fun for the entire family as well as the lasses down at the local," she's no doubt thinking to herself.

Chapter 13
Hair Today Gone Tomorrow

It's Monday morning and the Dunton playing field is a seething mass of keyed-up pupils bustling about like ants at a picnic. Something has made them very agitated indeed, but what or who is responsible for the fracas I can't quite tell. Some kids are shaking raised fists in the air, others are yelling hotly, and every single one is silly with excitement.

"Get 'im," squawks one.

"Again! Go on, throw it again!" heckles another.

What's happening? I attempt to keep my balance while standing on tiptoes, but my view is limited to a rippling swell of greasy heads and shoulders. "Any idea what's going on?" I ask the tall, scrawny bloke with shaggy hair standing beside me. He drops his chin and skims his eyes over me briefly.

"Big fight!" he finally declares, but doesn't offer any details. A fight? How Neanderthal can you get? You'd think a few civilized centuries of tea and scones and indoor plumbing would have drummed that nasty instinct out of us by now. "Yeah, that Alf is giving that Bennie fella a good seeing to," jeers Scarecrow. "He may be small, but he's a wiry one!"

Alfie? John Bennie? The news couldn't be worse! I should have guessed it would come to this. The last big fight Alf was involved in got him suspended with a final warning, so I must stop this one before any teachers pull up. I don't have time to think it through and impulsively tuck my head into my neck, fold my elbows into my sides, hunch my shoulders forward, and shove with all my might. I ram and pummel my way forward like a rugby player heading for a try, seeking out the smallest gaps between bodies and miraculously squeezing through. Some kids look annoyed by my forceful intrusion, others barely notice, and after a few minutes of jostling I finally emerge ringside.

No longer faced with backs I can now see Alfie, who—apart from a thin trail of scarlet blood leaking from his nose—looks pretty much unharmed. John Bennie has not fared as well and his left eye has already swollen to the size and color of a plump juicy grape, which matches the nasty gash streaking his cheekbone. But his injuries don't appear to be slowing him down one bit and the two of them are swinging and rolling and tussling like madmen. The world and everything contained therein gears down to slow motion as I stand there, mesmerized by the kaleidoscope of body fluids being sprayed into the air. Even the grunts of the opponents and howls of the crowd seem to have decelerated to a muffled growl. The only drop of good news is that none of my other friends are involved in the brawl.

A movement in the crowd sidetracks my gaze. Toby suddenly appears from out of nowhere and nose-dives into the sliver of space separating the two snarling boxers. He grabs Alfie's T-shirt as if to pull him away, but John Bennie sees his opportunity and seizes a grim handful of Toby's thick, blond hair and starts yanking for all he's worth. He's fighting like a girl! Toby's face crumples in a painful grimace as he tries to twist his body free, but John Bennie has the upper hand and he knows it. He raises his right knee and aims it squarely at Toby's crown jewels. As the agonizing force of the impact bleaches my best friend's face I feel my insides stockpile enough rage and strength to tear John Bennie's head right off his shoulders.

"GERROFF!" I bellow. My body is coiled up and ready to pounce, but I'm way too slow and a mysterious figure is instantly there before me. The pair that became three has now become four, and it takes me a few seconds to twig that the newcomer clawing her way over John Bennie's back is actually Becky. How dare she? The Beast has come to rescue my Toby, and I'm too sluggish, dim-witted, and too damn late to do a single thing to stop her!

"Oi! What's going on here?" a bass voice booms. It's Mr Povey with Mr MacIntyre, miraculously swooping down on the chaos.

Like puppets with the same master Alf, John Bennie, Toby, and BB simultaneously turn to face the scowling teachers and drop their fists. "Don't worry, Mr. Povey. It's all sorted. . . ." Toby gasps in a voice that's a few pitches higher than usual.

Mr. Povey's gaze rests an almost imperceptible millisecond longer on Alf than on John Bennie. To a latecomer it might appear as if Alf, Toby, and you-know-who were ganging up on John Bennie, which is not the case at all. But unfortunately Mr. Povey's timing is in Bennie's— rather than Alfie's—favor.

"Right! My office . . . the lot of you!" he hollers, pointing a trembling finger at the four of them. "And the rest of you rubbernecks can bloody well get back to class!" he roars at the awestruck crowd. I've never seen Mr. Povey this angry before and almost expect steam to spew from his ears, just like it does in the cartoons. I've also never ever heard him swear—not even when Clever Trevor blew up the geography department with his homemade Mount Vesuvius.

The spectators disband and slowly start making their way back to class. Most of them appear rather bummed that their morning entertainment has come to an end. Toby and Alfie slink off in the direction of Povey's office and Beastly Becky teeters along with them, desperately trying to keep up. I feel like throwing my shoe at the back of her head. Both grown-ups wait for John Bennie to follow before bringing up the rear, which leaves me standing alone in the middle of the playing field like a lanced wart.

That's it! Toby will never forget that it was Becky and not me who came to his aid, which means that I really and truly have finally lost my best friend. What starts out as a small whimper in the pit of my belly begins to grow and swell and amplify in my lungs until my whole body is shaking with a long wail of self-pity and sorrow. I throw my head back and give it all I've got, feeling the fury and anguish pouring from me until my energy is drained and I'm emptied of everything. Thank my stars the playing field is already deserted.

Quote twenty-seven of the Good Sense Guide tells me to accept the things I cannot change, but how am I supposed to know when to finally give up on Toby? Am I just wasting time and energy hoping for the impossible? Perhaps I should be gracious and wish Toby and Beastly Becky all the happiness in the world, but I wouldn't mean it, which makes it a lie. Now, although I understand that telling lies is not the way to earn a first-class ticket to heaven, being a teenager has taught me that sometimes I'm going to have to tell a white lie or two (and perhaps even a grayish one here and there). But when it comes to telling tall tales I think I've finally figured out the Good Sense rule: "Never ever lie to yourself." It's all too easy to believe your own lies, and once you start you'll soon forget where the truth begins and where it ends, and that'll cause trouble in all shapes and colors. And if you're always truthful with yourself it should keep your conscience in tiptop shape and prevent you from telling serious humdinger-fibs to others. So no, I definitely cannot be happy for Toby and the Beast, but what I can do is try to accept the inevitable. Another thing I can do is channel all my energy into Cyclops, with whom I shall now attempt to fall hopelessly and completely in love. Never underestimate the power of the mind and positive thought. Just believing that you can is half the journey to actually succeeding. That's number eleven of the Good Sense Guide.

"So is it true?" a voice rumbles from behind me. I twirl around quickly to find Tom-Tom and his hair, which is thankfully already starting to grow back.

"Is what true?"

"Did Alf have a fight with John Bennie? That's what everybody's saying," he replies.

"If that's what they're saying then it must be true, although John Bennie did just as much of the fighting." I really don't know why I'm defending Alfie to Tom-Tom; perhaps defending Alfie has simply become a subconscious habit. "Oh, and Toby and his girlfriend got in on the scrap too. It was a real eye-opener," I add. I mean this in more ways than Tom-Tom will ever understand.

"Toby's girlfriend?" he pips, wrinkling up his nose.

I want to add something spiteful about girls that fight being tasteless and trashy, but I know I'm only being bitter because she got in there before I did. "This is going to get Alf expelled for sure," I say instead.

"Yeah, and it wasn't even his fight in the first place," Tom-Tom adds softly. I don't say anything to this and we set off on the walk back to class.

The corridors are quaking with news of the big fight and everyone appears too busy trading titbits of gossip to notice that we're seriously late for class. Both Tom-Tom and I have Mr. Povey's French class next, but judging by the rumpus coming from his classroom he must still be busy playing referee with Mr. MacIntyre. It's about time luck was on our side.

World War III has broken out inside the classroom and we have to dodge airborne stationery, chewing-gum missiles and inflated condom balloons to reach our seats. Somebody has written something extremely rude about Mr. Povey's mother on the blackboard in bold chalky letters, but for mental health reasons I have to believe that no one's mother would do that.

Frannie is in our French class and I scan the bustling bodies to see if she's already there, but without any luck. Pity, I was rather hoping the old reliable Frannie had come back to stay. Standing between me, Tom-Tom and our desks is Jimmy Hilliard, who is standing behind Martha Middleton and simulating a move from the Kama Sutra. The unfortunate Martha is trying her best to ignore the fact that he's alive and breathing the same air as her. A few of the kids follow Tom-Tom with goggle-eyed stares as if he's just climbed out of a cereal box, but for the most part our entrance goes unnoticed.

"I don't know if I can take five minutes in this zoo," I murmur to Tom-Tom as I quickly collapse in my chair to avoid the air traffic.

"Let's give it a few minutes. If Povey doesn't show then we'll leave," replies Tom-Tom. I'm nodding my head in agreement and secretly hoping he won't show when all of a sudden the noise level in the room plummets drastically. Drat! It must be Mr. Povey. But then somebody lets out a wolf-whistle, which springboards a hail of jagged comments.

"Hey, it's Mr. Baldy Wo-man . . . ," sniggers one voice.

"It's about time you came out the closet, Fran-K!" hollers another.

"You have a lover's tiff with a lawnmower, darlin'?" chirps the obnoxious Jimmy Hilliard.

I can't imagine what's electrified this lot. And that's when I see her. Frannie has finally arrived for class . . . and she's shaved her hair off. Instead of beautiful long, dark curls tumbling down her back, she now has a halo of stiff bristles sprouting from her shiny pink scalp. But Frannie appears unconcerned by all the attention she's receiving and heads directly toward Tom-Tom and me, where she takes her place at the desk in front of mine.

"Not a word about my hair!" she orders sternly, turning around to face us. "Are we straight?"

What hair? But Tom-Tom and I nod bleakly, our mouths gaping like Venus flytraps. Poor Tom-Tom is almost as white as me.

Chapter 14
Booby Trap

Dad is parked in front of the telly and tinkering with the video's remote control, which, although needing regular jiggle-abouts, still worked but is now completely dismantled. The coffee table is muddled with tiny gadgety-looking components and small colorful wires you just know will never be returned to their rightful place, but it keeps him occupied so we all remain quiet and accept that for a while we'll have to get up and operate the video machine manually.

In spite of "the mirror incident" (which I've tried to put behind me), Cyclops has sent me a text asking if I'd like to go and see a movie with him this evening, and considering that I have an empty calendar and I'm supposed to be falling in love with him, I decide to accept. After recent events I think I should just be grateful that somebody still wants to go out in public with me. I also decide to stop calling him Cyclops, because the name does not conjure up any visions of hearts and romance. This week has seemed doomed and peculiar and I really could do with some company and a good laugh, so I hope we see a comedy, because Glen's about as funny as an algebra exam. I arrange to meet Glen-previously-known-as-Cyclops at the cinema complex at six sharp, and I'm glad to see that he's waiting for me when I arrive.

"Hey, Ella," he grins and sets off a wink in my direction. Oh please, anything but the wink, I plead mentally, closing my eyes to erase the image from my memory. I think Cupid is on vacation because I don't seem to be getting any help on this love mission whatsoever. "I've already bought our movie tickets," he smiles again, "so why don't we go for a walk? We've got some time before the film starts."

Sounds harmless, so I nod. He thankfully doesn't attempt to hold my hand, and after a while I start to realize that I'm rather enjoying myself and Glen's company. He's proving easier to talk to than I expected and once he gets over trying to be so cool I find that he's really quite interesting. He tells me all about his family (but thankfully doesn't make any direct reference to See-mown) and his beloved Alsatian called Zoot (which I think is a funky name and much better than naff Trixie any day), and how he'd like to become a professional athlete one day.

Toby is going to be a professional footballer, my head squeals. If I'm going to succeed with my love mission I must join in this conversation and forget all about Toby-I've-suddenly-discovered-my-hormones-Sinclair. "So how are you enjoying living in Dunton?" I ask, trying to ignore the loud voices in my skull. This is hard slog. I wish I could just leave this romance business up to Mother Nature, although she did muck up the whole twin thing so maybe I'm better off steering this love boat myself.

"I miss the sea, but it's nice to have more family nearby," Glen answers. "Oh, speaking of which, did Pearl tell you that she's going on a date with that Tatty fella on Monday?"

"No, she didn't," I muse, "and why Monday? That's a rather strange day for a first date, isn't it?"

"You really do dissect everything, Ella Mental!" he smirks.

"Who said you could call me that?" I snap, preparing to attack.

"Er, sorry. That's what Pearl . . . ," he splutters, quite obviously wishing every letter of the sentence back into his mouth.

"Just because I like to think things through first doesn't mean I dissect everything. I happen to find thinking an excellent way of avoiding catastrophes . . . unlike some people I know." I am fuming and vow never to speak to Pearl again.

"I suppose so," he says, suddenly looking a little uptight. "Listen, I was only kidding about the Ella Mental thing. It's good to have an enquiring mind, I think it's cool."

"Stop changing the subject," I mutter icily, irritated by his agreeable attitude and feeling a little guilty about my flare-up. "Now what were you saying about Pearl?"

"Well that's about it really. We'd better get going or we're going to miss the trailers."

The cinema is surprisingly empty for a Friday night and it doesn't take us long to buy popcorn and sweets and find our seats. I adore going to the movies! When the lights fade and the film starts rolling I feel like I've been erased from existence and mutated into an invisible observer—a fly on the wall, where absolutely nothing is expected of me except to sit in the dark and to watch and listen. The pictures transport me to places and situations I couldn't visit or see or experience in a dozen lifetimes. I get so tangled up in the images

I usually even manage to disregard the noisy back-row blabbers.

I love almost everything about going to the cinema, except for the adverts. I especially hate the ones that tell me winged sanitary pads will transform my period into a cartwheels-of-joy experience. Who do they think they're fooling? Even Mother Teresa kicked the cat when it was that time of the month. These adverts are an insult to intelligent human beings everywhere. It's one thing watching these nonsense ads on telly at home, where you can get up and go to the loo or make a cup of tea, but I resent having to pay to watch them.

There's another thing I hate about going to the movies, and that's cinema snoggers. Take Lovelips and his girlfriend sitting directly in front of Glen and me, for example. Not only is it mortifyingly embarrassing for the rest of us to have to sit and watch and listen to their sickly spit-sucking, but I don't understand why they waste good money just to get off with each other. Why not go and do it somewhere free (like at home), where poor innocent strangers don't have to witness your rampant sex hormones? Thanks to Lovelips and his tongue tactics right now I'd like nothing better than to crawl under my chair and dissolve into the carpet, but I'm forced to make do with avoiding Glen's gaze instead. And I'm successful at this for close on thirteen and a half minutes. I know because I'm timing.

"Could I have some of your popcorn?" Glen suddenly whispers in my right ear.

Sigh. "Sure," I hiss. He could just stick his hand in and grab from the top, but instead he decides to lean right over me and peer inside the tub while he considers his options. This isn't a box of chocolates, I'm tempted to say, but stare transfixed at the screen instead. And that's when I feel something warm and heavy creeping across my back. I wish it were a giant slug, but I know that it can only be Glen's arm because his left hand is all of a sudden resting on my left shoulder. My blood freezes to the consistency of cherry slush-puppy and my heart begins to quiver and pound with the effort of pumping it around my body. I try to remain calm and act as if everything is normal, until I simply cannot take it any longer.

"Oops," I whisper, leaning forward and pretending to fiddle with my shoes. Glen's arm has no alternative but to slip from my shoulders and I remain bent over for a few blissful moments.

"My laces were undone," I explain sheepishly, once I'm sitting upright again.

"Ah," Glen murmurs, instantly transferring his arm from the back of the seat to my shoulders once again. So much for that ploy. I'm terrified he'll misinterpret the slightest movement I make as encouragement, so I sit there unmoving—surviving on tiny gulps of air like a stranded guppy. The harder I try to remain motionless the more I'm aware of my muscles nervously trembling and twitching. We remain sitting like this for what seems like an eternity, until eventually Glen misconstrues my immobility as a sign for him to take it to the next base. My only warning of what's to come is the brief flutter of movement caught out of the corner of my right eye, but it's not enough to prepare me for Glen's devilish daring. Like an eagle descending on unsuspecting prey his hand takes off from my shoulder and swoops down to land on my breasticle.

"Whaaat . . . !" I screech, swivelling around to face my predator.

"Oh, Ella . . . ," he swoons and mashes his lips against my gaping mouth, which causes our teeth to bash together painfully.

"Gerroffme!" I burble, trying to break free.

Now it's Glen's turn to get a fright and in his panic he squeezes my breasticle even harder.

"Have you lost your mind? What do you think you're doing?" I sizzle furiously and karate-chop myself free. "I am so out of here!"

"Wait, I'm really sorry, Ella," he stammers. "I figured . . . er, you know . . ."

"No, I don't know!" I spit. "But if you ever grope me again I'll pummel you like a punchbag!"

"Oi, you two, keep it down!" Lovelips turns around and commands.

"Listen, Tentacle Tongue," I bark back at the interfering stranger, "I had to listen to you sucking face all the way through the trailers, so why don't you just pipe down?"

"What did you say?" Lovelips fumes.

I'm not normally a confrontational person and I can't remember ever arguing with someone I didn't even know, but I'm getting just a bit fed up with everybody pushing my buttons all the time. "You heard me!" I yell back.

"We're trying to watch a movie over here," a female voice yaps from behind.

"Yeah, take it outside!" another voice adds.

"Do what you like," I say to Glen, "but I'm getting out of here!"

I don't think I've ever been so humiliated in all my life, nor do I want to do something I'll regret, so I escape the cinema and only stop moving when I'm finally standing beneath the glare of the streetlights. Glen is not far behind me and when he catches me up I can't help noticing that he's turned an unhealthy ashen color. He looks like he's seen a ghost. And that's when the absurdity of the situation hits home and starts me laughing. I set off with a neat girlie giggle that makes my shoulders quiver daintily, but this quickly grows into a chuckle, flowing stronger and harder until eventually I'm cackling hysterically and swiping at the tears that are splashing on my cheeks. At first Glen simply stares at me as if I've gone completely and utterly bonkers, but then he slowly begins to see the funny side of things too, which gets him sniggering, and very soon the pair of us are clutching our stomachs and rocking with gales of hilarious hooting. Bystanders gawp as if we're certifiable, but we're too busy laughing at ourselves to notice or care.

We eventually calm down and our laughter recedes, making room for a big, hairy, awkward moment. Glen doesn't seem to be warming up to saying anything so I decide to deal with the situation the only way I know how: with plain-spoken honesty. "I want you to know that I still think you're a decent bloke," I begin, "and I'm sorry if I led you on." Glen doesn't say a word so I blunder ahead. "You don't have to live up to your mates' expectations of you, you know. You really should chill a bit and ease up on the schmaltz, because who you are is so much nicer and a lot more interesting."

Glen looks at me earnestly and runs his hand through his hair. "Yeah, maybe—but we're not that different, you and me."

"What do you mean?" I ask warily.

"Maybe I do try to live up to the image my friends have created for me. Maybe I should be more faithful to who I really am, but look at you—you spend your life trying to please everybody. You're so desperate to be liked and accepted that you'll happily put yourself second all the time. Trying to impress everyone is not all that different to trying to please everyone, now is it?"

"That's so not true!" I object half-heartedly, although somewhere deep in my gut I know that he's right. I'm always putting other people first, even when they don't acknowledge or appreciate it. "Well . . . maybe we both just need a bit more time to figure out exactly who we are," I suggest in the end. "Maybe when we're sure of who we are we'll rely less on what other people think of us for direction and trust ourselves to be ourselves, huh?"

"Yeah, maybe," says Glen, staring intently at his shoes. "And maybe you also need to either get over Toby or sort it out, because while you sit around and wait and wonder you're just wasting everybody's time—including mine."

Glen's comment sucks the voice from my thoughts. How can he possibly know about Toby? Am I that transparent? Worse yet, if Glen's figured it out—how many other people know that I'm secretly in love with my ex-best friend? This is heavy stuff.

"Oh, and Ella?" he adds, suddenly grinning.

"Yes?" I answer timidly, afraid of what's to come.

"That's a mean left hook you've got!"

Chapter 15
Shaken But Not Stirred

It's a new week at Dunton Secondary and the word is out: Alf has been expelled for—as Mr. Povey puts it—"repeatedly causing the sort of disturbance and disorder that stands between the pupils of Dunton and their basic right to an education." Povey talks about rights, and yet John Bennie walks free!

School is becoming more horrendous with each passing day. Toby and Becky have been united by their first official warning and although she still spends her breaks with Maddy Pierce and the rest of the Dunton bimbos, she makes a point of popping up at regular intervals, swanking past our group in a skirt that's rolled up at least twice at the waistband. I'm grateful for the fact that Toby doesn't behave any differently when she is around, although he's still treating me as if I scarcely exist. And Frannie is still angrily sporting her spiky stubble and threatening to vandalize anyone who mentions it. It's adios to Alfie, I can't help feeling that Tom-Tom is in denial about the incident in the boiler room, and Pearl is, well . . . still the same old Pearl. We both have PE with Miss Wickström after break and right now I would gladly swap a body part for a sick note or some foolproof excuse to blag my way out of it. My threadbare "I'm not feeling well" and "it's that time of the month" excuses no longer work because Miss Wickström has started keeping a record of when each girl has her period. I'm certain that this is a violation of our human rights, but she says she's fed up with everyone using "that old excuse" all the time. So not only am I forced to freeze my rear off in unflattering running shorts that reveal my wobbly bits in all their glory, but my girlie breasticle bits have grown and reached the stage where any physical activity gives them a life of their own. Wobbly bits and pointy bits; the life of a teenage girl is not easy.

The boys have a different PE teacher and are supposed to have an entirely separate class to ours, but it never ever works out that way and we always end up huffing and puffing on the field alongside one another. So as if displaying my various bits to the world isn't bad enough, I've also got to cope with the drooling boys ogling my—

and every other girl's—bouncing chest. Physical Education? Physical Torture, more like it!

Pearl arrives just in time to hear Miss Wickström informing us that Mr. Mellor—who is the boys' PE teacher—is off with the flu, so we're all playing a game of volleyball together: girls against boys. Why doesn't she just slip a noose about my neck and get it over with? Perhaps she enjoys my suffering.

"I'd rather eat a crushed glass sandwich," I moan at Pearl, whose shorts are so tight it looks like she's nicked them off her sister's Barbie.

"Stop whinging, Ella Mental Watson," she breezes, doing a few warm-up star jumps in front of the slobbering boys' team. She's more than happy to have a combined PE class.

Has she no shame? "Why are you so chipper?" I bleat.

"Today is the big date!" Pearl sings gleefully, squeezing out a little high-pitched squeal at the end. "I'm finally meeting Tatty!"

Ah, right. How could Pearl, Tatty and their dopey date be anything other than the first thought on my mind? "So where is he taking you then?" I ask, reluctantly performing limbering exercises with the other kids but completely disregarding Miss Wickström's explanation on the benefits of a good stretch.

"We're meeting up at his tattoo parlor," she titters, "and he's going to give me my first tattoo for free! Well, it's not really his tattoo parlor, he only works there but he sort of runs it and can do what he likes."

"You're getting a tattoo?" I gasp in astonishment.

"And about time too!" she confirms, confidently reaching for her toes. "I'm having an apple bound up in razor wire tattooed on my neck—just below my right ear. It's meant to symbolize the apple Eve was given in the Garden of Eden, and the razor wire represents the years of subjugation and repression we women have endured as a result."

For a moment I think Pearl's having me on, but then I see the self-satisfied look on her face and quickly realize that she's being as straight-up as a telephone pole. "What . . . but . . . are you serious?" I blither, suddenly forgetting all about Miss Wickström and the PE class. And since when does Pearl use words like subjugation and repression?

"It was Tatty's idea," Pearl reveals. "And course I am! I need a change, and you know what they say—a change is as good as a holiday!"

Yes, except a tattoo is for life, not just a holiday, I privately panic. But reasoning with Pearl is a bit like licking your elbow: not only is it practically impossible, you feel stupid for even trying. So I remain quiet and simply fall in line as Miss Wickström herds us in the direction of the volleyball net where the wide-eyed boys are already waiting and eagerly anticipating a half-hour's worth of jump shots and over-arm volleys.

I think I'm going to need help with this Pearlodrama, so after PE I text Glen and ask him to please meet me outside the gates after school. I say that it's urgent and far more important than anything else he may have planned for the afternoon. I'm sure that will rouse him into action. With that done I attempt to concentrate on my final lesson of the day, which is Biology. I'd really like to listen to Mrs. Sidwell's heartfelt babble about photosynthesis, but I can't help succumbing to a delicious dream about the good old times when fearless Toby would arrive to save the day. Glen's okay and I definitely won't ever call him Cyclops again, but he's still not Toby, who lately spends just about all his time with Tom-Tom. If and how Becky fits into all of this I simply have no idea. Everything that was familiar and a crucial component in my life has metamorphosed into something unrecognizable right before my very eyes. I suppose in a way I should be grateful for Pearlodramas; at least something has remained constant.

When I finally escape Mrs. Sidwell, I find Glen, true to form, waiting for me outside the school gates. "What's up?" he asks. The flesh on his forehead is puckered with concern.

"Thanks for meeting me," I say haltingly, suddenly questioning whether this was such a good idea. I hope he hasn't misinterpreted my text. "It's about Pearl," I say, eager to make things clear. "She's actually going on a date with that Tatty bloke!"

Glen squints at me. "Wasn't I the one who told you that?"

"Yes, but guess where they're going?" But I don't wait for him to guess. "They're going to his tattoo parlor, and he's going to give her a tattoo . . . on her neck . . . an apple wrapped up in razor wire that's meant to symbolize women's lib or something daft!"

"Mmmm," Glen shakes his head soberly. "Not like the good old days any more, is it—when popcorn and a movie was considered the perfect first date." Then he laughs and gives me a teasing wink.

"Er, yuh—whatever," I mumble. "But the date is not really the point, now is it? Did you hear me—I said she's going to have her neck tattooed!"

"Nah she won't!" Glen shrugs.

"She told me herself!"

"And you want me to . . . ?"

"I think we should catch them up and stop her from doing something stupid that she's bound to regret!" I declare emphatically. "Because she will do it, you know."

"So you want us to go along on their date then?" Glen asks, his eyes sparkling mischievously. "Ella, if you want to go out with me you should just ask."

"Ha ha," I fake-laugh and grimace. "No, I don't want to go on their date, nor do I want to go on a date with you. No offence, of course."

"None taken. Of course."

"So I wonder which tattoo parlor it is then?" I speculate out loud.

Glen remains silent with his palm pressed against his mouth. I think he thinks I think he looks thoughtful, but I can quite easily see that he's trying to cover up the enormous smirk plastered across his mug with his hand. No Oscars for that one, cheezoid!

"Aarrgh!" I blare at him. "I'll go on my own you big . . . you big . . . er . . . CYCLOPS!"

"Wait a minute, Ella!" he says, seizing my hand. "I'll come with you, okay? Just calm down."

"I'll calm down if you start taking this a little more seriously," I gripe. "She is your cousin!"

"Okay fine—but I've got a quick and easy solution to this problem," he says.

"You do?"

"Yup, and the solution is my mum—I believe you've met her?" He pauses after he says this and grins so broadly his dimples almost disappear into his cheeks.

"Just get on with it!" I order, feeling the heat spreading across my face. Pearl obviously gets her blabbermouth from See-mown.

"You've heard of the Godfather, right? Well, in our family we have the Godmother, and that's my mum. None of us would dare cross her—and she'll soon put Pearl straight. I'll get her to phone Pearl's mobile, okay?"

"Er, great," I reply, feeling just a little deflated. I had geared myself up for a much bigger event.

Chapter 16
Love 'n' Hate

Don't get me wrong, I couldn't be happier about the outcome of Monday's shenanigans, but right now I'm feeling suffocated by this recent landslide of madness surrounding me. Or maybe I'm generally just fed up and feeling down. I hope that sooner or later Pearl stops looking for love in all the wrong places, although I somehow doubt it. I don't especially blame or judge her for it; I'm just getting a bit tired and bored of it all. My friends all seem so needy and misunderstood at the moment; even plod-along Frannie has mutated into some entirely new and mysterious creature. It seems to me that to be misunderstood is just part and parcel of being human. We're all too different to ever completely understand one another anyway, so maybe we should all just take up bowling instead. Of course I want to support my friends as much as I can, but by my calculations I'm about due for some receiving—instead of just giving all the time. What happened to the Golden Rule: Treat others as you would have them treat you (also Good Sense Guide number six, by the way)? When is someone going to save me?

Just when I decide to give up on mankind and spend the rest of my days wallowing privately in my own self-pity, Tom-Tom arrives to restore my faith in my fellow man. And his timing could not be better.

"You okay?" he asks. Right now I'm slumped over my homeroom desk with my school blazer draped over my head so that the morons in my class don't disturb me, but even though I can't actually see Tom-Tom's face I recognize his voice immediately.

"Yes, I guess so." My muffled misery penetrates the heavy material of my blazer. "It's nothing I could explain, anyway."

"You could try," replies Tom-Tom, gently lifting the blazer from my head. The fresh air is wonderfully cool—it was getting rather hot inside there.

"No, I couldn't," I answer. "Everything is just fine, honest."

"I heard that you saved Pearl's neck—literally!" he enthuses, trying his best to fluff up my feathers.

"Yahoo whatever," I exhale noisily. "Pearl is a

big girl and one of these days she has to start thinking for herself. And when I say 'for herself,' I don't mean 'about herself,' because we all know that she manages that just fine."

"So you and Glen are quite the heroes, huh?" Tom-Tom adds.

"Glen Shmen!" I'm sulking. Great, that's just what I need—for Tom-Tom to think that Glen and I spend our afternoons hanging out together, keeping the streets of Dunton safe for small, furry animals and egghead teenagers!

Tom-Tom doesn't mention Glen's name again and changes the subject entirely. "Toby is trying out for the Under Fifteen Firsts footy team and I said I'd go along and support him. Do you want to come?" He obviously doesn't know about my Toby troubles. Don't blokes ever talk amongst themselves?

My ex-best friend used to appreciate having me on the sidelines, but that was in the good old days before Beastly Becky jostled her way on to the scene. I'd give anything to be near him again. "Er, I guess so," I say casually, as if I'm not bothered either way.

We reach the footy field to find Toby already kitted up and doing warm-up exercises. He raises his hand in greeting when he sees us, and even though he's probably actually only waving to Tom-Tom I've got a good imagination and pretend that the wave was meant for me too. If Toby is surprised to see me then he doesn't show it, which is just like a bloke. They're such control freaks. And I'm a typical girl: emotional silly putty in his hands. Just the sight of him sets my blood swirling and eddying in my veins until I feel quite light-headed.

"Trials start at quarter to," the Under Fifteens coach broadcasts loudly to all the kitted lads bouncing about around him. The players fan out and begin booting balls to each other and practice-shooting at the goals. I expect Toby to join them, but he starts walking in our direction instead. I've rehearsed this encounter a thousand times in my head already, but still I feel mentally unprepared to face him.

"Hey, Tom-Tom," he says, wiping away the sweat on his top lip with his shirtsleeve. Oh no, he's just going to ignore me. I should have expected this. "How are things, Ella?" he then adds, turning in my direction. My world goes topsy-turvy and I suddenly forget how to breathe. If only I'd washed my hair this morning.

"Hi, Toby," I croak. I'm not sure where to

lean my eyes so I shuffle about like a simpleton instead, looking everywhere but at him. I know that later I'm going to regret not handling this better, but right now I'm simply concentrating on remaining conscious.

"Those other guys any good?" Tom-Tom thankfully comes to my rescue.

"Yeah, some," Toby says with a wonky grin, which sets my insides bubbling like a hot spring. "What have you been up to, Ella?" he asks, kneeling down to re-tie his bootlaces.

Um . . . what have I been up to? At this very moment in time I cannot recall a single thing I've done. Ever. In my whole life. Seeing Toby this close up has deleted my brain's entire inbox.

"Ella?" Toby repeats, now looking at me a little oddly.

"Er, gosh . . . where to begin?" I mumble. "Anna's been grounded in the Garden of Eden . . . because, um Fran, you know, is bald with photosynthesis thanks to Lovelips who was in the cinema just before the big fight with the beast."

Both Toby and Tom-Tom remain silent for a time, uneasily trying to decipher my garbled sentence.

"HEY, ELLA!" a voice unexpectedly hollers

from somewhere to my right. Normally I would be grateful for the interruption, but this voice sounds ominously familiar. "How are you doing?" It's Glen, and he's breathless from running. "Didn't you hear me calling you? Guess not. Well I just wanted to tell you that the movie is showing for another week and seeing as we only got to see half of it last time, maybe you'd like to go with me again this Friday?" He gives me a knowing wink when he mentions us only seeing half the movie last time, as if we'd been smooching or something for the other half.

"I'll get back to you, okay?" I say aggressively, desperately wishing he would just melt into the ether.

"Yes, er okay then." He looks a little wounded by my terse response but thankfully turns back in the direction of the changing rooms. He did that on purpose, I rant inwardly. He saw me talking to Toby and he did that on purpose! I suppose I shouldn't forget that he is Pearl's cousin, so what else was I expecting? That's one family that could do with a little more chlorine in their gene pool.

I spin around to find Tom-Tom standing alone; Toby has rejoined the rest of the football players on the field.

Chapter 17
Reality Bites!

It's our mum's birthday and Anna and I have been hauled off to the Jewel Garden—Mum's favourite restaurant—to "celebrate" (or the Watson version thereof). Unfortunately the restaurant is not in Dunton, so not only do we have to endure a boring family dinner, but we've had to suffer a twenty-minute car journey just to get here. Then of course there's the twenty-minute drive home again, so basically we're spending an extra forty minutes with the parental units than if we'd just gone to any one of the perfectly fine eating establishments in our area. And that's presuming there's no traffic. They don't call the M25 the biggest parking lot in the world for nothing. Trust our mother to fancy Japanese food! Why can't she be like the rest of the mums I know and be content with good old-fashioned Italian? Mama Mia's is not five minutes up the road. Better yet, Pizza Express delivers. Of course Anna and I have tried everything from lying about imaginary homework to straightforward begging in order to get out of going, but Dad was having none of it. So here we sit—jammed into a window booth at the wretched Jewel Garden, which smells like an aquarium in need of a filter change.

I'd rather waste away than eat whiffy raw fish and the only thing I can find that's vaguely edible is called *tori no mizutaki*—number twenty-four on the menu, which is described as a type of chicken stew. I'm not convinced, but at least it's cooked and I order it without much gusto. Anna and Dad are more daring (or is it dippy?) and both settle on some raw pickled seafood dish with fermented soybeans thrown in for good measure. What's the point of inventing fire if you're not going to use it? And hello, has everybody left their taste buds at home?

We sit there for the next hour, making small talk and munching on our unpronounceable exotic dinners. The words "just the bill please" are all I can think about throughout the entire dismal experience and I want to hug our dad when he finally utters them.

Wasting precious little time I'm halfway into my coat and almost out the front door when I suddenly glimpse Toby's dad sitting just a few meters away from me. His table is dressed in fresh flowers and a romantic candle, which illuminates his face as he gazes serenely into the eyes of his female dinner companion. Now he's taking her hand and leaning forward to press a seemingly endless kiss into her upturned palm. Her ruby-painted lips blow him a kiss in return and then release a string of dainty giggles that fill the air between them like music. As I stand there staring in on their intimate moment with my jaw trailing the floor like some Peeping Tom, I can't help wondering how Mrs. T would feel about her husband canoodling with this strange blonde woman.

"Do you think you could move it up, Ella? Some of us would desperately like to get home!" Anna yaps in my ear, impatiently waiting for me to exit the restaurant.

"Anna, look!" I gasp, nudging her in the direction of Toby's double-dealing dad and the non-Mrs.-T woman.

"At what?" Anna is irritated, just as eager as I was a few seconds ago to get out of here.

"Look, it's Toby's dad! And he's with another woman! A woman that's definitely not Toby's mum," I gulp.

Anna takes a few seconds to do the maths but

188

is typically less than sympathetic about the total. "Yes, well there's nothing I can do about it," she snaps. "And there's nothing you can do about it either, crazy girl. So just keep walking and act like you haven't seen a thing, before the parental units catch on and delay our departure from this fishy funeral parlor."

I'm too traumatized to resist and allow Anna to bulldoze me forward until we're out in the cold biting air of the Jewel Garden's car park.

"Well, wasn't that just lovely!" Mum exclaims merrily as she climbs into the driver's seat of our old Vauxhall.

Dad just quit his job as a representative for a local chemical company to start a home-industry business making organic bar snacks with Norm-From-The-Pub. He says organic is the way to go, although I can't imagine it makes much difference when you're poisoning your body with alcohol anyway. Luckily the "home-industry" side of things happens at Norm's house and not ours, but that doesn't change the fact that dad is broke and mum had to pay the bill for her own birthday supper.

I remain quiet and subdued for the rest of the journey home, thinking about this explosive information I've been handed. I'm gutted. Now I know how detectives working for the bomb squad feel: One wrong move and this could all go off with a nasty bang and hurt a lot of people—one person in particular. How this ends is up to me, although I really don't feel up to taking a ride on this new and altogether terrifying emotional rollercoaster. Mum and her cursed Jewel Garden! It's thanks to her that I'm in this mess in the first place.

I bought Mum a miniature birthday cake with the sentiment Enjoy Your Special Day spelled out elegantly in icing on its roof. When we get home she wants us all to have a cup of tea and a slice of the cake before we turn in for the night, but I'm feeling too nauseous and upset to eat anything. Not even cake.

"What's wrong, Ella? It's not like you to pass up dessert. Are you feeling sick?" Mum asks me.

Oh blah blah . . . not like me to pass up dessert. I'm not Porky Pig. "I'm not feeling well," I answer truthfully. She doesn't need to know that my queasiness is emotional rather than physical. I heave myself upstairs to the haven that is my bedroom and along the way happen to catch Dad muttering the words "Ella . . . sulky . . . ungrateful," but I don't care.

I always thought that adults held the answers to life's questions, but the older I get the more I realize that they're just as confused and have just as much to figure out as we do. But at least we don't go around pretending we know everything. Er . . . or if we do then at least we don't force other people to listen to our crackpot advice.

I know I'm having a nervous breakdown when I'm too distressed to eat, and there's only one thing for a nervous breakdown: a whirlwind cleanup. The exercise leaves your body exhausted and the resulting tidiness clears your headspace so that your troubles appear just as logical and ordered as your surroundings. So I start with my CD rack and return each disc to its correct casing; I buzz through the stack of papers and magazines cluttering my desk—binning what's out of date or useless or boring; I move to my cupboard and hang up all the clothes that have just been bundled up and carelessly rammed into shelves. I even find my missing Dodgers hoodie. Once that's done I survey my room with itchy fingers, wondering what I can attack next.

I still haven't discovered the reason behind Anna's transformation into a couldn't-care-less Lady Muck, but it's beginning to annoy me. How I wish I could have my sweet, prissy Anna back—the one who would spend hours curling her hair, matching her outfits with her underwear and plotting strategies for the next fashion sale. Why do we only appreciate things when they're gone? All I have are a bunch of unanswered questions, so perhaps it's time I had it out with my sister and popped the lid on her bizarre behavior. And I've got a bad mood brewing and I'm ready to boil, so there's no time like the present.

I'm strategically relying on the element of surprise to get Anna talking and purposefully barge into her bedroom without knocking. I find it empty. She must be downstairs eating cake and watching telly. But the desire to meddle is still with me and I'm unable to resist taking this opportunity to have a bit of a poke around. And anyway, the chances of Anna opening up to me are about as good as me having a Top Ten hit, so perhaps snooping really is the only way to get to the bottom of the mystery that is Anna Watson.

When Anna and I were much younger we shared absolutely everything except for a few top-secret, prized possessions which Anna kept hidden in an old biscuit tin in a nook at the back of her cupboard. I never knew that the biscuit tin, the prized possessions or nook even existed until our eighth birthday when, in the excitement of celebrating her own birthday, Anna forgot that it was my birthday too. I had given her my favorite hairclip, so as her gift to me Anna decided to show me her hush-hush hoard. That's an impressive gift when you're a curious eight-year-old. Of course Anna made me promise to keep my eyes squeezed tightly shut while she extracted the tin from its very special hiding place, but she made such a huge fuss about it I was unable to resist sneaking a peek through my fingers, which is how I came to discover the nook. Her prized possessions turned out to be a long-dead ladybird, some foreign coins, a moldy square of our (now divorced) aunt's wedding cake, a key to who-knows-what, a purple bird feather and a tube of half-used crimson lipstick that must once-upon-a-time have belonged to our mum. Since that day I've never once considered snooping in Anna's cherished biscuit tin. Until today, that is: I don't even know if the tin still exists, but right now it seems as good a place as any to search for the loose end that will hopefully unravel my twin's secrets.

Anna's cupboard is already half-open and after pushing aside her hanging clothes I begin exploring the cupboard wall with my fingers, looking for a small recess. It's not nearly as straightforward as I thought it would be, but just when I'm about to give up my hand suddenly disappears into nothingness. I've finally found the nook, and there's something cold and metal perched inside. It's the biscuit tin, although it's a lot smaller than I remembered. How sweet that Anna kept it for all these years!

For an old tin the lid prises off surprisingly easily, but there's not a ladybird or lipstick in sight. Instead of precious trinkets I find an almost-full packet of Craven A Menthol cigarettes, a folded envelope, a dried pressed flower, a brochure for a kibbutz in Israel, and what looks like one of Mum's old shoulder pads that's been cut into two wads of what—I'm guessing, judging by their size and shape—can only be bra padding. Ha, I knew it was unnatural for one twin to have bigger breasticles than the other! I dip into the tin and remove the envelope. Inside is a letter covered in tilting, squashed-up cursive. It's dated almost two months ago and is addressed to Anna.

Dear Anna,
Thanks for your letter. I'm flattered you feel that way about me. Yes, we've known each

other for a while and we do have a good time together, although I'm not so sure that we're quite what you call a couple. Of course I like you, but it's not that simple. I think I'm only being fair & honest when I say that we come from very different worlds. To get to the point-there are times when you say and do things that well, let's just say that they make me look silly and make you stand out. If you really want this to go further (like you say you do) then you really need to fit in with my crowd. The most noticeable difference is the way you speak. You've been around me enough to know what I mean. We do and say things a certain way. I'm sure you'll pick it up if you try and watch closely. See you on Saturday.

Spence x

Like a game of Tetris the missing pieces suddenly tumble into place, building a clear and true picture of my sister's life. But how could she let herself be insulted and bossed about by this poncy pig head?

"What the blazes do you think you're doing?" Anna screeches from the doorway. I didn't even hear the door open.

"If I were you I would not be throwing a hissy-fit," I counter in a voice that's astonishingly slick and cool.

"Why are you going through my things?" Anna snarls through clamped teeth.

"I've been worried about you," I reply curtly, sounding decidedly school-marmish. "You've been acting very strangely ever since you started going out with that space-cadet Spencer and now I finally know why." I replace the lid on the biscuit tin and toss it on her bed, not giving a sausage who might see it. "I can't believe you let him treat you that way! Where's your self-respect, Anna Watson? He may have pots of money, live in a mansion and go to a fancy-shmancy school, but he's no better than you or me."

Anna is white with rage. "What would you know about it . . . or anything, for that matter, Ella Watson!" She hisses in reply. "And get this straight: just because you're my sister does not mean you have the right to go through my things and poke your big pointy nose in my business!"

Big pointy nose? "Well somebody has got to stop you acting like a freaking idiot!" I sputter furiously. "'He could be the one' . . . blah blah. I can't believe you! Grow a backbone. You think you're so cool, Anna—but now it's my turn to be ashamed to be your sister! Pah!"

Astonishment renders Anna's feet and tongue immobile and she stands there gawking as I stomp past her and out of the room. Talk about having absolutely no sense at all! Anna is so definitely getting the very first copy of the Elemental Good Sense Guide when it's published.

Chapter 18
Red Letter Day

Try as I might to take one day at a time, every so often a bunch of them come along and knock me down in one go. As if seeing Toby's cheating dad wasn't dreadful enough, the visit to the Jewel Garden has left me sick with food poisoning and serenading the toilet bowl for the past twenty-four hours. And Anna and I are, of course, once again looking right through each other. It seems as though my life has finally hit rock bottom, but instead of being completely depressed about it I really feel like a weight has been lifted from my shoulders. There's a strange sense of peace that goes with the certainty that things simply cannot get any worse.

I've been paging through my diary for inspiration and I keep coming back to Good Sense Guide number seven which says: Never let the fear of failure be an excuse for not trying. Society tells me that to fail is the most terrible thing in the world, but I know it isn't. Failure is part of what makes us human. What would be much worse is if my fear of failure stopped me from trying at all. It's up to me to get Toby's parents back together again. Fate led me to the Jewel Garden so that I could save my best friend's family and win him back and that's what I'm going to do. And when Toby discovers my good deed he'll realize that I'm worth a zillion Beckys and forget she exists. This time *I'll* be Toby's hero.

So feeling oddly upbeat, I sit down at my neat and ordered desk, determined to come up with a revolutionary solution to the quandaries I'm faced with. There's no way I can tell Toby, his mum, or Daftcow Melanie about the fateful scene I witnessed at the Jewel Garden, and it certainly wouldn't solve anything anyway. I suppose I really should go to the source of the problem, but I have no idea who the non-Mrs.-T woman is. I somehow don't think she's from Dunton; our town's just too small to guard that kind of secret for very long. I could, however, tackle Toby's dad with the news that he's been caught out. I could ask him to stop his cheating and threaten to expose him if he doesn't. In my mind's eye this seems like the perfect plan, but in reality I know that I don't have the nerve to do it. But I won't be beaten; I've watched enough daytime television to know that an anonymous letter is the perfect way to deliver this sort of damning threat. I'm no Patsy Pushover.

With masses of *CosmoGIRL!* back issues to put to good use I plough through my desk drawers, searching for scissors and a tube of glue. I also need a sheet of blank paper to stick the letters to, and I'm careful to choose the bottom sheet of my foolscap pad—knowing that it won't have any visible imprints from any previous writing I've done. Handwriting is like a fingerprint and can be easily traced. It takes just over thirty minutes and four issues of *CosmoGIRL!* to complete my letter, and once I'm done I scrutinize my work with a jumble of fearful pride.

Dear Mr Sinclair
i KNOw wHat YOu DiD Last
SatUrDaY nig#t! i was at t#e JeweL
GarDen anD i saw YOu wiTH t#at
WoMaN. YOu are a MaRRieD MaN
anD t#e Fat#er Of twO
CHILDren, anD even if ONe is a Daft
COw YOu stiLL s#OuLD nOt Be

CHEATING ON YOUr faMiLY. SO YOU
BeTTeR STOP OR i WiLL TeLL.
HOnest. i aM nOT afraiD TO TeLL.
reaLLY i aM nOT. SweaR.

I leave it unsigned because I think it adds an element of mystery to the letter. Plus it's supposed to be anonymous, so signing it really would defeat the object. A surge of adrenalin bullets through my veins as I relish my first taste of a cheap thrill.

But how do I deliver it to Toby's dad? I need to make sure that nobody else opens the letter before him, especially not Toby, his mum, or whatchamadingy, so I can't risk delivering it to the Sinclair home. I do, however, know where Toby's dad works and it's not far from our school, so I suppose I could address it: "MR SINCLAIR: PRIVATE AND CONFIDENTIAL," and slip it into the office postbox early one morning. But I can't risk using *CosmoGIRL!* cuttings for the envelope—that would make other staff members at his office suspicious—so I print the words with my left hand to ensure that the writing is untraceable. Ha, I laugh in the face of danger.

That's the double-dealing cad of a dad problem out the way. I suppose that if I'm going to be a meddling busybody I may as well give it all I've got, and so I head off to our local clinic and stockpile various pamphlets and information packs on Sexually Transmitted Diseases and teenage pregnancy (rumor has it that Pearl is now dating let's-get-hammered-Lars.) At first the nurse on duty is quite helpful, but after my fifth request (I thought I might also collect some information on the dangers of smoking as well as donating your body to medical science) she glares at me warily. I try to reassure her that I'm personally only interested in becoming a body donor and that the rest of the pamphlets are for my friends. I also attempt to tell her about the Elemental Good Sense Guide, but she snubs me with a belittling smile and frog-marches me out of her waiting room.

I wait until the following day to play postie and deliver the assorted bits of paper to their rightful recipients. First I pop Mr. Sinclair's letter into the company letterbox that stands directly outside his redbrick office building. During break time I drop a handful of pamphlets into Pearl's schoolbag (it's pointless handing them to her personally—she'll only scoff at my good deed). After school I have just enough time to stop off at the library and by the time I reach home I find that Anna is already covering the couch and watching telly with Dog snuggled up close to her side. Dad's revised list of house rules has obviously had a big impact. I know I should probably take the tactful approach when dealing with my touchy twin, but I've had a bellyful of being tactful. Instead of tiptoeing around her and choosing my timing carefully, I strut straight up to her.

"Are you over yourself yet?" I ask, tossing a paperback library book at her. It lands cover-up and both sister and pet glance at the title and then eyeball me indignantly. It's a self-help book called *Loving You for You: A Guide to Growing Your Self-Respect*.

"Oh please, Anna—you're not the victim here!" I screech, instantly irritated by her expression. It's not easy saving people from themselves. "And as for you Dog, just remember who saved you from Bruiser the killer bull terrier. You're both big bleedin' girls!"

Anna continues to stare at me as if I've just thrown pigswill at her and then tips her eyes heavenward. I'm not stupid enough to think that she's actually going to try to see some sense, but I am hoping that good sense will find her. "Whatever!" she finally mutters, and turns to face the television once again. She's too stubborn to pick the book up while I'm around so I head upstairs to wade through the cheerless stack of homework I've been handed. I find it rather peculiar how Anna and I are in the same year and yet she's always got her nose in the telly guide while my "big pointy" nose is permanently stuck in some tedious, picture-less textbook.

Today may have been productive, but I've still got two more dilemmas to work through. The first is Glen. There's no way I'm going to a movie, to Mars, or anywhere else with him (the love mission has been aborted), but in a strange way I do now sort of consider him a friend. I mean, he was quite helpful with the neck-tattoo Pearlodrama. And to be honest, I would probably be a lot nicer to Glen if Toby didn't exist, which really isn't fair if you think about it. It's unfair even if you don't think about it. It's not right to be nice to someone one day and then wish him or her away the next. I hate it when people do that to me. Remember: Always treat others as you would have them treat you. So with that advice firmly in mind I decide that sending letters is a cowardly yet effective way of dealing with a problem, and one that may just work with the Glen situation too. Only this time I don't think I'll go the anonymous route or annihilate my *CosmoGIRL!* back issues. For once I actually have airtime on my phone, so I'll send a text instead.

HI GLEN. SORRY IF WAZ RUDE THE OTHER DAY. TX 4
THE INVITE. HV LOTZ 2 SORT OUT. NEED SPACE
&/OR TIME.
PLUS WE MAY B MOVING TO SRI LANKA. HOPE U
UNDRSTND & WE CAN STILL B FRIENDS. OK BYE. ELLA.

I almost put "Love Ella," but then decide that it's probably not a good idea. I want to keep things simple, although I don't suppose the spineless flash of inspiration about a possible move to Sri Lanka is keeping it simple. I press the send button anyway.

My second dilemma is Frannie Mendes. I wish her mystery was hidden inside a biscuit tin and that all I had to do was find its hiding place, but I know it's not going to be nearly that easy. Deep in my gut I know that something really bad has happened to make Frannie behave this way. I haven't forgotten my promise to Maria Mendes either. I gave her my word that I would try to crack the code to Frannie's sadness, but I simply have no idea how to go about it. All I can do is ask, and I've asked a thousand times already. Since her tennis-ball haircut I'm not even allowed to ask any more, so all that's left is for me to make sure that I'm around when she does finally decide to uncover her secrets. It's a pity the clinic didn't have any pamphlets on "mysterious gloominess"; I would've got a whole bucketload for Frannie.

Chapter 19
Kindred Spirits

I know I need to give Anna enough space to think things through for herself and for the next few days we simply stay out of each other's way. Right now Pearl, Tom-Tom, Fran, and I are sitting together in the school quad, lounging like lizards in the noon-time sunshine and gossiping about trivial things. It almost reminds me of the good old days, before everything flipped out. For the first time in a long time I feel carefree and liberated and I don't want to think about anything that carries a consequence. Alf and Toby are the only ones absent, although Frannie says that Alf has settled into his new school and has already found a new group of mates, so maybe he doesn't really count as absent any more. That'll be a first. And as for Toby, I really hope he'll show up soon.

Tattoo-less (and consequently Tatty-less, we're guessing) Pearl is her usual insufferable, know-it-all self and has been rattling on about moronic Lars for the past eleven minutes and twenty-seven seconds. She still hasn't uttered a peep about the clinic pamphlets I secretly left for her, although I suppose there's a good chance she hasn't even looked inside her schoolbag yet. As long as her makeup case is within fumbling reach Pearl really has no interest in whatever other items may be lurking within her schoolbag's murky interior. On Planet Pearl reality is a bit like scoffing pizza: You pick out the interesting bits and leave the boring crust for some other poor soul to clear up afterwards.

After school I find myself home alone for the first time in ages. Just as I'm settling in to some peace and quiet the front door opens and slam-bangs shut with a bone-shaking boom.

"Thanks a lot!" roars Anna as she thuds her way past me into the kitchen. Considering that there's no one else about I can only presume that this is sarcasm with my name on it. I remain on the couch—immersed in MTV. But the blissful silence doesn't last long and is quickly broken by a brutal whack, only this time it's the cupboard door that's being mistreated. Suddenly Anna appears before me, equipped with a chocolate bar and a seriously scratchy attitude. She doesn't say anything and simply stands there glaring at me.

"What?" I say defensively.

"Spencer dumped me!" she cries. "And it's all your rotten fault."

"What do you mean it's my fault? I've never even met the guy," I snap in defense.

"I told him that it was my turn for ultimatums and that he had to like me for me or not at all. And he went for the not at all option! He said that if I couldn't mix with his crowd then he'd rather I didn't mix with him," she adds, flopping down on to the couch beside me. "So that's it. No more Eppingworth and no more Spencer."

"Right . . . ," I say slowly, wondering which she'll miss more, Spencer or Eppingworth? "You've definitely done the right thing though, Anna. Just remember: You are your own person! Freedom of choice—that's what elevates us above wild animals!"

"Pleeaase! No quotes from the Elemental Nonsense Guide. Not now!" she wails. "I don't think my nerves could take it."

"That's actually Tom-Tom's gem. But, you know, if you took a few tips from the Good Sense Guide once in a while you wouldn't date twerps like Spen. . . ." I begin, but the threatening crease growing between Anna's eyebrows is a warning that if I value my life I should probably stop right there.

"So now will you stop harassing me?" she growls.

"Well, I guess so . . . sure, why not. What are sisters for?"

"And, Ella?" she ventures.

"Yuh?"

"I'm not ashamed that you're my sister," she says softly. "We're twins for jeepers-creepers sake and I sort of, you know...love you." We both sit there with glowing cheeks, looking uncomfortable with this unexpected closeness that's sprouted between us.

"Er, me too," I falter. I feel like I may cry, but this time it's not from sadness or frustration. This time it's from happiness.

There's a weird pause of togetherness.

"Anna, could you give me some advice?" I ask, eager to test out our new bond.

"Sure, go ahead."

"It's Frannie," I begin uncertainly. "I think there's something seriously wrong with her, but I don't know what it is. She just won't open up to me and I'm scared that if I don't do something to help her things will only get worse."

"Mmm . . . ," Anna hums, wading through my words and her thoughts. "Well, the only thing I can think of is reverse psychology. You know; turn the tables on her by pretending that you have a problem you need help with. That might get her to open up."

"That sounds like a good idea. But what do I say to her?" I ask, excited at the prospect.

"Make something up if you have to. Maybe what's stopping Fran from talking is her fear that no one will understand whatever it is she's going through. So you have to somehow convince her—without actually knowing what her problem is—that you would understand. I bet everyone is bright and breezy around her because they hope it will make her feel better and get her to talk, but it probably only makes her feel worse."

Thinking back on my visits with Frannie reminds me that this is exactly how I behave around her. And I'm sure I'm not the only one. Anna has a point, and a very good point: Frannie needs to see me as a kindred spirit, not as some gung-ho holiday camp co-ordinator. "You're a genius!" I declare, squeezing my sweet sister tightly. It's time for me to do the talking.

Chapter 20
Bursting Boils

Feeling bolstered by Anna's support and unwilling to risk waiting another day to confront Frannie, I decide to head for her house immediately. For once Maria Mendes appears indifferent to my arrival and dejectedly points me upstairs, her sad eyes signalling that Frannie is once again holed up in her bedroom. I scale the stairs two at a time and tap insistently on the familiar white door. "Frannie, it's Ella, can I come in?"

"Uh, yeah okay," a gruff voice murmurs from within.

Instead of the familiar pale floral wallpaper Frannie's bedroom walls have been painted a deep berry color, making the room appear dark and smaller than usual. "Nice walls," I mumble dully, purposefully trying not to look too interested. Frannie is still dressed in her school uniform and tucked up under the bedcovers watching television.

"Some clueless new game show," she says, thumbing toward the screen. "Wanna watch?"

"Nah, not really," I sigh, trying to get into character and really feel the grief. "I'm a bit low, actually," I say and then remain quiet for a moment or two. I'm hoping my somber mood will prick Frannie's disinterest. "Any chance of a chat? You don't have to say anything; I just really need an ear."

"An ear?" she hesitates, squirming deeper into her nest. "Er, I guess so."

"Maybe it's better if we go for a walk," I suggest, tightening my grip on Anna's plan. Frannie may be more willing to talk if her mum isn't pacing just one floor away.

"A walk?" Frannie whines incredulously, as if I've just suggested that we riverdance naked down the High Street.

"Yes, you know . . . to the park perhaps? I wouldn't mind some fresh air," I say, trying to look doe-eyed and desperate.

She eventually sighs and rouses herself reluctantly from the bed. "Right, okay fine then."

If Maria is surprised to see Fran out and about she doesn't say anything and we set off on a slow walk in the direction of the park. The sun is diluted but bright enough to warm our bones and the air is tangy with the spices of autumn. I'm finding it rather difficult to appear solemn—autumn is a magical time of year. I love it when the light and leaves are glowing and golden and the chill gnaws away nature's old, used skin so that in spring she can grow a beautiful, brand new one. That's teamwork for you.

As we amble along I casually start to tell Fran about Anna and Spencer, and for the first time in a long time I actually get a reaction from Frannie. Not a full-size reaction, but her eyebrows lift ever so slightly and her face puckers in surprise. Her response spurs me on to confide in my long-lost friend. I feel like we have so much time to make up for and before I know it the words start gushing from me like a high-pressure hose. I tell her about Anna; I cry about poor Tom-Tom; I laugh about my encounter with groping Glen; and finally—without even planning to, I tell her how I kissed Toby and lost Toby in one fateful day. My unburdening takes almost twenty minutes and Frannie listens patiently and silently, her facial expression shifting with each slice of news. When I'm eventually done she stares at me with a look of bleary-eyed wonderment, like someone who has just woken from a long, deep sleep.

"Whew, where have I been?" she finally

gasps, running a hand through her bristly dark hair and settling into a corner of the park bench.

"I don't know, Frannie, where have you been?" I say quietly, hoping I don't sound too pushy.

"I've got some stuff to tell you too, Ella Mental," she sighs, staring out at nothing in particular. "It's been eating me up from the inside out and I don't think I can handle it on my own any more." Her arms are locked around her raised knees protectively and when her gaze eventually returns to find mine her eyes are glossy and wet. I am paralyzed; too terrified to breathe or twitch a muscle.

"My uncle has moved back to England from Portugal," she says quietly. I already know this, but I don't dare utter a word in case I say the wrong thing and she buttons up her lips forever. "He used to live here, you know. Years ago, until I was about eight years old. We're a close family and my mum and uncle are probably the closest of the lot, so he used to visit us all the time." Her sentences are short and disjointed, as if she's painfully squashing the words out of her mouth one by one. "Everybody thought he was the best uncle in the world. He used to babysit me all the time—he loved spending time with me, he said.

215

And that was when he did things to me, usually at night and in my bedroom when no one was around."

My blood turns frosty and my fingers and toes start to tingle with the painful cold that's seeping through my bones and tissue. I don't want to hear this. I want her to stop telling me this right now. It's already too much, and more than I ever thought it could be. Somebody needs to hear this, just not me.

But Frannie doesn't stop and her voice scrambles higher and faster instead until it sounds like it might snap in two. "He would climb under the covers and touch me in places he had no right to. And I would cry and plead with him to stop. I even stopped wearing my nightie to bed and slept in jeans and a shirt instead, but it made no difference. He even thought it was 'cute.' It's weird, you know, but when you're a little kid you really aren't sure what's normal and what's not. There's not much you can compare it with. Just how do you tell what's right and what's wrong? I mean, my mum and dad loved my Uncle Mannie. They welcomed him into our home, so in my childish mind I figured that what he was doing must be okay. For a while I even thought he was doing it with their permission. Of course he said all the usual stuff—that it was private and special, but it never felt special. It just felt disgusting." She spews this last sentence out of her mouth like it's bitter and venomous.

For the past few minutes Frannie has been staring intently at her hands, but now she raises her gaze and zones in on me—as if daring me to be repulsed and run away from her and the ugliness. I remain unmoving and do my best to balance her stare. Her look is intense and flits frantically between anger, panic and confusion. I'm consumed by her terrifying revelation but still my emotions seem pathetic and trite next to hers. It feels like the ultimate betrayal, until I realize that it's impossible for me to feel all that she feels. Today I am the lucky one.

"And so one Christmas I confided in my grandfather," she continues. She sounds detached, like she's reading me a story. "I told him that Uncle Mannie was touching me in ways that hurt and scared me. I said I was sorry if I was doing wrong by telling because it was supposed to be a secret, but locking it up inside me was giving me nightmares. I didn't say very much else and for a few minutes my grandfather didn't say very much either. He listened with an empty face, not seeming particularly angry or sad or . . . anything really. Then he took my hand and said that if I loved my mum and dad and wanted to keep our family together I would never ever tell another soul. He said it was just for the two of us. But he meant the three of us, didn't he? He meant him, Uncle Mannie, and me.

"Uncle Mannie boarded a plane and flew back to Portugal the very next day, which is where he's been living for the past six years. My grandfather must have put Mannie on that plane; that was his way of dealing with the problem, I suppose. And I did the only thing I could: I shoved it all deep inside me and pretended that I was a normal, happy kid. But my grandfather died a couple of years ago and now dear old Uncle Mannie has returned to England, like nothing ever happened. Nobody knows our secret, but seeing him again has given life to all those memories I worked so hard to smother. Frankenstein's monster has been raised from the dead and is once again eating me alive, bit by bit by bit."

Two bloated, unbroken streams of tears have snaked a path from the corners of her dark eyes down to her chin, and I watch them spilling over on to her jumper like copy-cat waterfalls. And I say a prayer to God, pleading with Him to send me the right words that will make her pain bearable. But as hard as I pray no words come and my mind remains silent and bare and useless, although my heart is full—and maybe that's enough for the moment. Perhaps silent company heals quicker than words of advice.

"It's good you told me, Frannie," I eventually whisper, gathering her into my arms and rhythmically rubbing her soft spiky head. Is this why she's been working so hard to camouflage her loveliness? "From this moment on it's all going to get better; this is the beginning of the end of all your pain and sadness. Everything is going to be all right. Nothing can change what happened, but you'll never be alone with it again." My voice has subconsciously taken on a sing-song quality, as if I'm crooning her to sleep with a lullaby.

When we finally prepare to leave the park and return home Frannie turns to face me earnestly. Her tears have dried but her face is still pale and stained with salt. "You must tell my mum," she says, clutching my fingers tightly. "I can't. So you must."

"Are you sure, Frannie?" I ask, feeling

dreadfully sick at the prospect. "You don't think it would be better coming from you?"

"No," she insists, as if she won't hear another word on the subject. "I simply can't. This is going to hurt her too much."

This last sentence helps me to understand things better. "All right then," I say quietly. "I'll do whatever you need me to do." But I sound much braver than I feel.

When we reach her house Frannie immediately takes off for her room and I find Maria sitting quietly on the couch in the lounge, waiting for me. I have no idea how she guessed that today was the day Frannie would burst her boil, but she's guessed correctly. And she's waiting, looking nervous and eager at the same time, fearing the worst but well aware that nothing can be worse than not knowing. Her small brown hands flutter nervously in her lap. She reminds me of a fragile bird waiting to be fed. I'm not qualified to do this, the voice in my head cries over and over. This is too big. This is just too big. I wish I could say anything—absolutely anything in the whole wide world except the words I'm expected to say right now. I sit on the couch beside her and put my hand over her own. The silence sickens me and my throat stings with the sour taste of bile.

I try not to think as the words tumble from my mouth, exactly as Frannie spoke them, but in less detail. There are certain particulars Maria does not need to know. I feel oddly detached from the situation, as if I'm an outsider looking in through a window, and I observe how her gentle face changes with every sentence I speak. Her first reaction is one of disbelief: Her eyes widen and bulge and her mouth stretches into a freakish O shape. I desperately want to shut up this instant, but I somehow can't keep my lips from moving and the words from falling. It's like I'm on auto-pilot, hypnotized by the chaos. I've made promises to Frannie and Maria and detaching myself is the only way I'm able to keep them. The burden of this is just too heavy to do it any other way.

Maria's disbelief is quickly chased by a surge of shock that freezes her distorted features and jams her movements. For a few moments it seems as if she's stopped breathing, but then suddenly her hand yanks from mine and hurtles towards me, stopping mid-air and trembling just a few inches from my face. I don't flinch. Not because I'm brave, but because I'm simply too stunned to move. Her kind face is consumed by an animal rage; she desperately wants to believe that I'm lying—that this is all a figment of my twisted imagination and that the monster is really me, instead of her beloved brother. When the staggering reality of the situation finally makes an impact her face implodes with pain and grief, her dark eyes—Frannie's eyes—clouding over in a glaze of misery. She remains sitting for a few minutes, like a broken doll, just staring at me. Her bent mouth quivers and tries to express the hurt that's blazing inside her chest, but her jaws remain rigid and unresponsive. Finally a soft wail warbles from her taut lips and she leaps to her feet and runs for the stairs that will lead her to Frannie's bedroom.

I feel a sense of relief at her departure, but not for myself. It's much better that Maria asks Frannie the desperate questions that are making her dizzy; the sharing will start the healing. I take this as my cue to leave and walk home from the Mendes household in a stupor. Right now I don't know what to think or feel; I'm too overwhelmed by the afternoon's events. Frannie and her mum and dad need time to mourn and vent, but I know they'll pull together and make it through in the end. They love each other too much not to.

I reach home and head straight up to my bedroom, sliding beneath the safety of my duvet and falling instantly into a deep, dreamless sleep. I'm not sure how long I sleep for, but I'm eventually woken by the telephone, which is ringing shrilly and bouncing about in its cradle. Like a remote-controlled robot I climb out of bed, pick up the handset and mutter something unintelligible into the mouthpiece.

"Ella?" a male voice utters.

"Uh, yuh," I mumble.

"Ellie, it's Toby. My dad came home to collect his things. He's moving out and never coming back again. Do you think you could come over for a bit?"

Chapter 21
Chicken Soup

I spend the duration of the walk to Toby's house fighting back the surge of nauseating guilt that's threatening to sink and drown me. This all my fault. Thanks to my stupid anonymous letter my poor friend has lost his dad. He may have been a big cheat, but as parental units go he could have been a lot worse. Why couldn't I just leave bad enough alone? I'm going to have to tell Toby, there's no other way around it. No matter how sad or angry or Miss-Fix-It I felt at the time, I am responsible for my actions. That's Good Sense Guide number nineteen. Luckily I'm too frantic with worry to fully comprehend the toll my friends and their giant-size problems are taking on my already fragile mental state, and I arrive at Toby's house to find him perched on the front step aiming stones into the birdbath.

"Hey, Tobes," I murmur, standing over him uncertainly. Should I give him a hug? What is the appropriate reaction to the news that your best friend's dad has chosen a bleached bimbo over his own flesh and blood?

"Melanie and my mum have gone to visit my grandparents, but I really wasn't up for it," he says, taking another pot shot at the birdbath. "Tea?"

Yes, tea—that's exactly what we need right now, and I bob my head vigorously. We both remain silent while Toby moves about the kitchen assembling the hot drinks, which we then take upstairs. Nothing much has changed in his bedroom and the blue linen, football posters, and trophies remain exactly as they were the last time I was here. The familiar continental pillow has been placed in front of the CD player, just like old times, and there's music spilling softly from the speakers. Toby walks over and drops to the floor, placing his head to one side of the continental pillow as if it were the most natural thing in the world. I put my tea down and do the same, carefully slotting my head in closely beside his. I can't believe how much I've missed this. I just wish the circumstances were different.

"I want you to know that I think I can deal with it," he says straight away, as if he's been waiting to unburden.

225

"That's good." I presume he's referring to his dad's departure.

"And I want you to know that I don't hold it against you," he adds.

Oh my goodness, he knows! He knows I wrote the anonymous letter! But how? At least he forgives me. Oh crikey! What do I do now? "You don't?" I stutter guiltily.

"No, I don't. I have no right to tell you what you can and can't do," he clarifies.

"Er . . . well, I guess not. But I want you to know why."

"I don't need the mucky details, Ellie. I know about the birds and bees, remember . . . I take biology too," Toby grunts.

Mucky details . . . the birds and the bees? He must be referring to his dad having the hots for the non-Mrs.-T. "Er yes, good. But I think we should still talk about the letter."

"What letter?" Toby asks.

"Uh . . . the letter you were just talking about?" My voice has definitely shot up a few pitches.

"I wasn't talking about any letter. I was talking about you and Glen. I want you to know that I've come to terms with the fact that you've got a boyfriend and I don't hold it against you. I don't

226

want it to come between us any more. You've chosen Glen and I think I can finally accept this. You're my best mate Ellie, and at the end of the day what matters is that you're happy."

"It does?" I squeak miserably.

"Yes, it does. Now, what's this letter you're talking about?"

"Nooooo!" I wail. "You can't be happy that I'm with Glen, because I'm not—and never was! Well, except for that one kiss and the . . . argh, never mind! Anyway, after you and I kissed you said it was a big mistake and then ignored me for weeks!"

"That's because you pulled away from me when I kissed you!" Toby exclaims, sitting bolt-upright and facing me. "What was I supposed to think? I felt really stupid and embarrassed, so I just said that it was a mistake. And if you pulled away then it obviously *was* a mistake."

"But I only pulled away because I couldn't breathe," I shriek, feeling both exasperated and elated by the discovery that there may still be a chance for Toby and me. "I wasn't expecting you to kiss me and my head was at a really awkward angle, but you never gave me a chance to explain and then you said it was a mistake, so I presumed . . . ! Ugh! And then you and Beastly Becky started getting all chummy . . . I even came to visit you one day and Daftcow Melanie told me that Becky was upstairs in this very room, so I just left you to it."

"Becky? Becky arrived on my doorstep uninvited. She may have been interested, but it was never a two-way thing. Nothing ever really happened; I guess she just thought there was more to it," Toby explains. "So what about Glen?" he adds, carefully rearranging all the pieces to create a clear picture of what really happened.

"It's a long story, but all that matters is that he and I are just friends and nothing more. That's all we've ever been!" I whoop.

"So you didn't hate my kiss then?" Toby asks with a silly grin decorating his face.

"No! I really loved your kiss," I admit shyly.

"Well, that's pretty cool then," he says, still grinning like an idiot.

"Before you say anything further, I think I should tell you about the letter I wrote to your dad," I say nervously. I can't risk getting my hopes up only to have them flattened when Toby discovers what a meddling brat I am. So I begin my story at the Jewel Garden and tell him everything, up to and including the shredded back-issues of *CosmoGIRL!* Toby's face drops at the mention of his dad kissing the non-Mrs.-T in the restaurant, but he recovers and quickly camouflages his unhappiness. As I recount the details of the anonymous letter his rigid jaw starts trembling. He's obviously furious and for a few terrifying moments I consider scampering out the front door, but the trembling turns to twitching, which grows into a smile and miraculously snowballs into hysterical laughter.

"Oh, Ella Mental!" he howls, wiping the tears from his eyes. "Your heart may be in the right place, but your head certainly isn't!"

"So you're not angry with me?" I ask hopefully.

He shakes his head. "My dad would have left eventually anyway. And he's been making a fool out of my mum, so I'm glad this happened sooner rather than later. But thanks for caring enough to at least try to do the right thing." And with that he leans forward and gently takes my chin in his hand, bringing my face towards his. Only this time I don't choke or pull away, and our kiss is long and sweet.

Lying on the blue continental pillow (post-kiss) and warmed by the knowledge that Toby—

my BOYFRIEND!—is just a touch away, I ponder the turbulent past months. I must admit that being a teenager takes some getting used to. I certainly feel more mature, but growing up is not all it's cracked up to be. It's unquestionably a lot more interesting, but it's also a lot more complicated and there's just so much more that can go wrong. The good news is that I'm starting to like myself more and learning to focus on my good—rather than my bad—points. So what if I'm not the skinniest, smartest, or funniest girl at Dunton Secondary. I have the telephone number for Pizza Express memorized by heart; I can always find Wally; I don't use electrical appliances in the bath; I'm never rude to waiters; I can pick up things with my toes; and my biggest crime is nicking Helen Shrosbury's Winnie the Pooh pencil when I was seven. I've learnt that liking myself is far more important than being liked by other people, and I've made that Good Sense Guide number thirty-two. I think this may just be the most important one yet. And so what if my home life is far from perfect? Just because our dad doesn't love us the way we want him to doesn't mean he doesn't love us with all he has. Things can always be worse.

Another thing I've figured out is that you can get through anything if you have people who care about you. It doesn't matter who, just as long as you have someone. I'm responsible for my own happiness, and it all comes down to a positive attitude and making the right choices. These are a few more lessons from the Elemental Good Sense Guide. As Winston Churchill once said: "The price of greatness is responsibility." Some people, like Pearl, just seem destined to do things the hard way, but if I learn from my mistakes I imagine things will turn out OK in the end. And if I get stuck, I'll always have the Elemental Good Sense Guide to turn to. Oh, and *CosmoGIRL!*, of course.

DISCARD

Peabody Public Library
Columbia City, IN

DISCARD

About the Author

Amber Deckers grew up in South Africa where she studied film, before going on to work for an advertising agency. During this time, she studied journalism part-time and eventually joined *Marie Claire* as a features and fashion writer and book reviewer.

Deciding to swap the shores of Africa for London, Amber worked for various publishers in London before joining an independent film production company with the idea of creating a television program about teenager issues. When the project was shelved, Amber decided to put her research and ideas into a novel, which is where this book came from.

Amber and her husband, Craig, have recently returned to the UK after living in Grenada. They now live on a farm in Kent with their Doberman called Blue and Calypso their tabby—both rescue animals from the West Indies. Amber works as a freelance journalist and is putting the finishing touches to her next novel.